致敬译界巨匠许渊冲先生

许渊冲译
杜甫诗选

SELECTED POEMS OF DU FU

编译

许渊冲

中国出版集团
中译出版社

目录

Contents

译序

梁启超在《情圣杜甫》一文中说：杜甫是当之无愧的情圣，“因为他的情感的内容是极丰富的，极真实的，极深刻的。他表情的方法又极熟练，能鞭辟到最深处，能将它全部完全反映不走样子，能像电气一般，一振一荡地打到别人的心弦上。中国文学界写情圣手，没有人比得上他，所以我叫他作情圣。”

杜甫生于公元712年。开元盛世孕育了中国文学史上的黄金时代。杜甫早年漫游四方，写出了“会当凌绝顶，一览众山小”(《望岳》)这样气吞山河、反映盛唐气概的名作。他和李白、高适等人结交，又写出了“李白一斗诗百篇，长安市上酒家眠”(《饮中八仙歌》)等感情洋溢、脍炙人口的诗篇。

公元755年，安史之乱爆发。他全家逃难，颠沛流离，目睹了人民生活的艰难困苦，写下了著名的“三吏”“三别”，这是那个时代社会动乱的真实写照。如《垂老别》中的“老妻卧路啼，岁暮衣裳单”；《新安吏》中的“白水暮东流，青山犹哭声”；《石壕吏》中的“存者且偷生，死者长已矣”。梁启超说：“这些诗是要作者的精神和那所写之人的精神并合为一，才能作出。……他作这首《垂老别》时，他已经化身作那位六七十岁拖去当兵的老头子；作这首《石壕吏》时，他已经化身作那位儿女死绝、衣食不给的老太婆，所以他说的话，完全和他们自己说一样。”

在安史之乱中，杜甫家在羌村避难，他一人去灵武，途中被叛军抓了去，写下了著名的《月夜》和《春望》，表达了他爱国爱家的思想情怀。从叛军中逃出后，他回到羌村，写了《羌村》三首，描述了当时的离乱生活。梁启超说：“他处处把自己主观的情感暴露，原不算写实派的做法。但如《羌村》《北征》等篇，多用第三者客观的资格，描写观察所得来的环境和别人情感，从极琐碎的断片详密刻画，确是近世写实派用的手法，所以可叫作半写实。这种做法，在中国文学界上，虽不敢说是杜工部首创，却可以说是杜工部用得最多而最妙。”

公元760年春天，杜甫流落到四川成都，投靠故人严武节度使。这时，他写了景仰诸葛亮的《蜀相》：“出师未捷身先死，长使英雄泪满襟。”也表达了他自己以身许国的胸怀。他在成都浣花溪畔修筑了草堂，描写草堂风景的名句有“窗含西岭千秋雪，门泊东吴万里船”，描写草堂生活的有《客至》：“花径不曾缘客扫，蓬门今始为君开。”草堂屋顶被风吹破，他又写了著名的《茅屋为秋风所破歌》：“安得广厦千万间，大庇天下寒士俱欢颜！”梁启超说：“因为他对于下层社会的痛苦看得真切，所以常把他们的痛苦当作自己的痛苦。”

公元765年，杜甫因为严武去世，失去依靠，携家离开了成都草堂，流落到长江三峡西头的夔州（今重庆奉节）。在这里，他写了著名的七言律诗《秋兴》和《登高》。这些诗把眼前景和心中情紧密地联系起来，情景交融，被认为是古今七律之冠。

杜甫写诗“语不惊人死不休”，《登高》中的一联可以说明：

无边落木萧萧下，不尽长江滚滚来。

这两句诗对仗工整，内容深刻，“无边落木”象征了唐王朝由盛转衰，“不尽长江”则象征了诗人对“开元之治”的怀念，希望荣华盛世随着滚滚江水又流回来，这种怀念在《秋兴八首》中表现得更多，但表现的不一定是现实的内容，而是艺术化了的情意，不但是内容超越了现实，形式也超越了传统的句法，如著名的一联：

香稻啄余鹦鹉粒，碧梧栖老凤凰枝。

这两句诗不好理解，因为诗中的主语和宾语换了位置，正常的位置应该是：鹦鹉啄余香稻粒，凤凰栖老碧梧枝。意思是说，“开元之治”政治开明，经济丰收，香稻遍地，余粒连鹦鹉都啄不完，可见其多；梧桐遮天蔽日，碧空万里，连凤凰都栖息在梧枝上，老了也不肯离开，可见安乐。那么，诗人为什么要颠倒主语和宾语的位置？因为诗人怀念的是香稻和碧梧，如果把鹦鹉和凤凰当主语，那就是喧宾夺主了。所以他宁可主宾颠倒，可见他认为内容重于形式，所以就改变句法了。这样做可以摆脱传统格律的拘束，使格律成为工具，而不必破坏格律的形式，来求得格律的超越。这种超越就是象征主义的新发展，用意象来表达感情，超越了现实，对后人的影响很大。因为这种意象化的表现比平铺直叙的现实描写更容易引起联想，给人更丰富的感受。这样，杜甫就影响了李商隐，试读《锦瑟》中的二联：

庄生晓梦迷蝴蝶，望帝春心托杜鹃。
沧海月明珠有泪，蓝田日暖玉生烟。

李商隐用来表现意象的景物和杜甫有所不同：杜甫用的落

叶、江水、香稻、碧梧，都是现实中所有的景物；而李商隐用的意象，如庄生的晓梦、望帝的春心、明珠的泪、暖玉的烟，却都是假想的事物。这表明了李商隐心灵的敏感比杜甫更加精细，更进一步。叶嘉莹在《论杜甫七律之演进及其承先启后之成就》一文中说：杜李“二人有一个共同的特色，那就是感情的过人，虽然二者的感情之性质并不尽同。杜甫是以其博大溢出于事物之外，义山（李商隐）则是以其深锐透入于事物之中。杜甫之情得之于生活的体验者多，义山之情则得之于心灵之锐感者多”。由此可以看出杜甫和李商隐的异同，也可以看出杜甫对后人的影响，以及后人对唐诗的发展。

公元768年正月，杜甫离开了夔州，漂泊到江陵（今湖北荆州)、岳州（今湖南岳阳)、潭州（今湖南长沙）等地。在江陵，他写了《江汉》一诗:“落日心犹壮，秋风病欲苏。古来存老马，不必取长途。”抒发了他怀才见弃的不平之气和报国思用的怀抱。在潭州，他遇见了流落江南的著名乐师李龟年，写出了“落花时节又逢君”这句总结时代沧桑、人生交往的名句。落花时节既表明了时令，又象征了李龟年的潦倒、杜甫的落魄、大唐王朝的衰落，含意非常丰富而又深刻。

清代金圣叹评点六才子书，认为第一才子书是《庄子》，第二是《离骚》，第三是《史记》，第四就是杜诗，第五则是《水浒》，第六是《西厢记》，由此可以看出杜甫在中国文学史上的地位。今天看来，《庄子》和《离骚》可以算是浪漫主义作品，李白继承发展了庄骚的文风，成了浪漫主义大诗人。《史记》和杜诗则是现实主义的代表作，开启了《水浒》及后来的现实主义一派。

Translator's Preface

Du Fu (712–770) was one of the greatest poets of the Tang dynasty, golden age of Chinese literature which could boast of its pastoralism of Wang Wei (701–761), romanticism of Li Bai (701–762), classicism of Du Fu, realism of Bai Juyi (772–846) and symbolism of Li Shangyin (812–858). Du Fu was called "Sage of Poetry" and his works "History in Verse", for his love of his country and his poetic art combined to make his poems vivid pictures of the life of his time and reflections of the thoughts of the people. While young, he travelled widely in the land and wrote the following verse at the age of twenty-four while gazing on the Tai Mountains:

Try to ascend the mountain's crest:
It dwarfs all peaks under our feet.

When he made friends with Li Bai, he wrote the following verse to show his admiration for his senior poet who was fond of drinking wine:

Li Bai would turn sweet nectar into verses fine.

During the rebellion of Tartar generals (755) he wrote many poems to show his suffering and the people's calamity, for example:

Have you not seen
On borders green
Bleached bones since olden days unburied on the plain?
The old ghosts weep and cry, while the new ghosts complain;
The air is loud with screech and scream in gloomy rain.

(*Song of the Conscripts*)

By the roadside cries my wife old,
So thinly clad in winter cold.

(*Lament of an Old Man*)

These verses, said Chinese critic Liang Qichao, proved what Keats wrote to be true: Beauty is truth and truth beauty. Liang also said the poem *Coming Back to Qiang Village* was highly realistic, forerunner of Bai Juyi's realism:

At my appearance starts my wife;
Then calming down, she melts in tears.
By chance I come back still in life,
While people drift in bitter years.

In 760 Du Fu came to Chengdu and built his thatched cottage, which he described in the following couplet:

My window frames the snow-crowned western mountain scene;
My door oft says to eastward-going ships "Goodbye!"

As for his life in the cottage, he wrote in the poem *For a Guest*:

The footpath strewn with fallen blooms is not swept clean;
My wicket gate is opened but for you today.

These lines show his love of secluded life as the pastoral poet Wang Wei. When his cottage was unroofed by an autumn gale, he wrote the following verse:

Could I get mansions covering ten thousand miles,
I'd house all scholars poor and make them beam with smiles.
...
Alas! Should these houses appear before my eye,
Frozen in my unroofed cot, content I'd die.

These lines show his love for the poor people and poor scholars. As for heroes and personages, we may read the last couplet of *Temple of the Premier of Shu*:

But he died before he accomplished his career.

How could heroes not wet their sleeves with tear on tear!

Du Fu's motto in versification was "never to stop short of surprising verse". For example, we may read his famous couplet in the octave *On the Height*:

The boundless forest sheds its leaves shower by shower;
The endless river rolls its waves hour after hour.

The fallen leaves may symbolize the decline of the Tang Dynasty and the rolling waves predict the revival of the past glory which the poet could not forget, for instance, in the following verse of *Reflections in Autumn*:

Parrots can't peck up all the grains left on the plain;
Phoenix when old on the plane tree will still remain.

Parrots and phoenix, grain and plane all symbolize the past glory. These symbols may be said to be forerunner of Li Shangyin's symbolic "Dim morning dream to be a butterfly". But grain and plane tree are visible while dim dream is not. From Du to Li we can see the development of symbolism in Tang poetry.

许渊冲译杜甫诗选

· · ·

望　岳

岱宗[①]夫如何?
齐鲁青未了。
造化[②]钟[③]神秀，
阴阳割昏晓。
荡胸生层云，
决眦[④]入归鸟。
会当[⑤]凌[⑥]绝顶，
一览众山小。

① 岱宗：指泰山，在今山东省泰安市城北。

② 造化：指天地、大自然。

③ 钟：聚集。

④ 决眦 (zì)：指睁大眼睛远望；眦，上下眼睑的接合处，指眼眶。

⑤ 会当：应当，定要。

⑥ 凌：登上。

这是杜甫诗中最早的一首，大约是公元736年杜甫24岁远望泰山时写的。诗开始说：这五岳之首的泰山多么高大，无边无际的青翠色覆盖了齐鲁两个古国（齐在泰山之北，鲁在泰山之南）。接着说：天地间的神奇秀美都凝聚在这里；泰山高耸入云，山南阳光灿烂，山北阴影朦

Gazing on Mount Tai

O peak of peaks, how high it stands!
One boundless green o'erspreads two States.
A marvel done by Nature's hands,
O'er light and shade it dominates.
Clouds rise therefrom and lave my breast;
My eyes are strained to see birds fleet.
Try to ascend the mountain's crest:
It dwarfs all peaks under our feet.

胧，仿佛是泰山把晓色和暮色分割开了。远远望去，山中云生雾绕，令人心旷神怡；一直望到天色将晚，瞪大眼睛看飞鸟归巢，眼眶似乎都要裂开了。于是诗人想到孔子“登泰山而小天下”的名言，心中思忖，总有一天，自己也要登上泰山的顶峰，俯视脚下起伏的群山。

题张氏隐居

（二首其二）

之子时相见，
邀人晚兴[①]留。
霁潭[②]鳣发发[③]，
春草鹿呦呦[④]。
杜酒[⑤]偏劳劝，
张梨[⑥]不外求。
前村山路险，
归醉每无愁。

① 晚兴：到傍晚还有兴致。

② 霁潭：一作“济潭”。

③ 发（bō）发：盛貌。

④ 呦（yōu）呦：象声词，鹿的叫声。

⑤ 杜酒：家酿的酒。

⑥ 张梨：原指张公大谷之梨，一种珍贵的梨树品种，后作为对梨的美称。

公元 736 年，杜甫游于齐赵，结识隐居的张氏，写下此诗。组诗共两首，第一首作于初识张氏时。这是其二，大概作于与张氏相熟之时，所以开首便道“之子时相见”。诗中含了很多典故，如“之子”直译过来是“这人”或“这位先生”，而《诗经》中有“彼其之子”句，汉成帝时有童谣“燕燕尾涎涎，张公子，时相见”。如此风趣地借用典故，不仅没有丝毫迂腐累赘之嫌，反而有些小小的幽默感，也表明二人的友谊情深。三、四两句状物，同样见于《诗经》，《卫风 · 硕人》中有“鳣

Written at Zhang's Hermitage

(II)

Although we have met now and then,
This evening I'm invited again.
Carps in the pool swim to and fro;
Deer on spring grass bleat high and low.
You urge me to drink my sweet wine;
No fruit is as your pear so fine.
Though rugged is my homeward way,
Drunken, my heart is ever gay.

鲔发发”，《小雅·鹿鸣》有“呦呦鹿鸣，食野之苹”之句。“鹿鸣思野草，可以喻嘉宾”，所以此联不单写景，更寓情于景，景中含情。“杜酒”句实打实是玩笑了，杜康是酒祖，所以称“杜酒”，这酒明明是我们杜家的造物，却劳动主家来劝饮。“张梨”是当时的名产“张公大谷之梨”，张氏的园中有梨，故也称“张梨”，既然这里有“张梨”，何必去外寻那个“张梨”。末联的醉行山路也不愁，映出了宾主尽欢的酣畅。全文将典故这般妙用，不可不谓“文章天成”了。

房兵曹胡马

胡马大宛名，
锋棱[①]瘦骨成。
竹批[②]双耳峻[③]，
风入四蹄轻。
所向无空阔，
真堪托死生[④]。
骁腾[⑤]有如此，
万里可横行。

① 锋棱：锋利的棱角。

② 竹批：形容马的耳朵像竹尖一样。

③ 峻：尖锐。

④ 托死生：值得托付生命。

⑤ 骁（xiāo）腾：勇猛矫健地奔驰。

此诗作于公元 740 或 741 年，杜甫本善骑射，也很爱马，写了很多咏马的诗。此诗前四句写的是马的品相，开首说马来自大宛，“大宛汗血古共知”，还未论及骨相，已然使人觉得这是一匹好马。接着写马的特征：骨骼嶙峋，耸如锋棱，耳如刀劈，尖锐挺立，都表明这是一匹良马。第四句由静转动，视角由旁观者到骑乘者，再现了神骏飞驰的场景，这很可能不是诗人的想象，而是真实的感受，所以才有下文的“真堪托死生”。有马如此，真可以横行万里，建功立业了。全诗写得豪放奔腾，饱含了诗人青年时期的壮志雄心。

The Tartar Steed of Captain Fang

A Tartar steed of famous breed
With bony frame runs at full speed.
As pointed bamboo its sharp ears,
Fast as the wind, light it appears.
Into nothing distances melt,*
No danger on its back is felt.
If their four hoofs can run their fill,
You can ride wherever you will.**

* Rewi Alley's version versified.

** Li Weijian's version versified.

画　鹰

素练风霜起，
苍鹰画作殊[1]。
㧐[2]身思狡兔，
侧目似愁胡[3]。
绦镟光堪摘[4]，
轩楹[5]势可呼。
何当击凡鸟，
毛血洒平芜[6]！

① 殊：不同凡响。

② 㧐（sǒng）身：即竦身，做好准备搏击的样子。

③ 愁胡：发愁的胡人。

④ 堪摘（zhāi）：可以摘除。

⑤ 轩楹：廊间的柱子，诗中指悬挂画鹰的地方。

⑥ 平芜：草原。

这是一首题画诗，大约与《房兵曹胡马》是同一时期作品。前两句为点题之句，洁白的画绢上，突然腾起了一片肃杀之气，以倒插起笔，读来令人讶异。第二句随即点明，原来是画中矫健不凡的鹰挟风带霜而起，带给人很强的视觉效果。三、四两句是传神之笔，由外而内，刻画出苍鹰搏击前的动作及其心理状态，仿佛眼前所见不是画，而是活生生的鹰。"绦"是系鹰用的丝绳；"镟"是系鹰用的金属的圆轴，分明是画，却明晃晃得照人，使人思忖着要把丝绳解掉，挂在轩楹上的俨然是活物，呼之欲出。最后直把画鹰当成真鹰，竟有任其搏飞高翔之愿，字里行间寄托着作者的思想和志向。

A Painted Falcon

A frosty wind from silk scroll seems to rise,
A superb falcon appears to the eyes.
It hovers to attack a cunning hare;
Like frowning monkey its side glances glare.
Its golden chains and rings brighten the hall,
Where it may alight to answer your call.
When would it strike the birds of lowly breed
And shed their blood and feathers at high speed?

兵车行

车辚辚[①]，马萧萧，
行人[②]弓箭各在腰。
耶[③]娘妻子走相送，
尘埃不见咸阳桥[④]。
牵衣顿足拦道哭，
哭声直上干[⑤]云霄。
道旁过者问行人，
行人但云点行频。
或从十五北防河，
便至四十西营田。
去时里正与裹头，
归来头白还戍边。

① 辚(lín)辚：雷声，比喻行车的声音。

② 行人：指出征的士兵。

③ 耶：通假字，同“爷”，父亲。

④ 咸阳桥：唐代时期是长安通往西北的必经之路。

⑤ 干(gān)：冲。

这首诗通过目睹耳闻的送别情景，揭露了唐玄宗对外发动战争给人民带来的痛苦，充满了反战情绪。诗从客观描写开始，说到“道旁过者问行人”，“过者”是过路人，就是杜甫自己；“行人”谈到15岁出征，40岁还在戍边的“征夫”。这句以上写诗人亲眼所见；以下写亲耳所闻：“行人但云点行频”，就是征夫回答说征兵太频繁了。下面的“武皇”是以汉喻唐，

Song of the Conscripts

Chariots rumble
And horses grumble.
The conscripts march with bow and arrows at the waist.
Their fathers, mothers, wives and children come in haste
To see them off; the bridge is shrouded in dust they've raised.
They clutch at their coats, stamp the feet and bar the way;
Their grief cries loud and strikes the cloud straight, straightaway.
An onlooker by roadside asks an enrollee.
"The conscription is frequent," only answers he.
Some went north at fifteen to guard the rivershore,
And were sent west to till the land at forty or more.
The elder bound their young heads when they went away;
Just home, they're sent to the frontier though their hair's gray.

用汉武帝影射唐玄宗,"汉家"也是暗指唐王室。"长者虽有问"一句中,"长者"是征夫对诗人的尊称,"役夫"是征夫的自称。"未休关西卒"是说还在大量征兵,要去关西打仗。这是诗人通过当事人的口述,揭露征兵和逼租给人民造成的苦难。最后,诗人用哀痛的笔调描述了战场上的悲惨现实。全诗运用口语非常突出,前人评说:"语杂歌谣,最易感人,愈浅愈切。"

边庭[①]流血成海水，
武皇开边意未已。
君不闻，
汉家山东二百州，
千村万落生荆杞[②]。
纵有健妇把锄犁，
禾生陇亩[③]无东西[④]。
况复秦兵耐苦战，
被驱不异犬与鸡。
长者虽有问，
役夫敢申恨？
且如今年冬，
未休关西卒。
县官急索租，
租税从何出？
信知生男恶，
反是生女好。

① 边庭：边疆。

② 荆杞（qǐ）：荆棘、枸杞，带刺的野生灌木。

③ 陇（lǒng）亩：田地。

④ 无东西：指不成行列。

The field on borderland becomes a sea of blood;
The emperor's greed for land is still at high flood.
Have you not heard
Two hundred districts east of the Hua Mountains lie,
Where briers and brambles grow in villages far and nigh?
Although stout women can wield the plough and the hoe,
Thorns and weeds in the east as in the west o'ergrow.
The enemy are used to hard and stubborn fight;
Our men are driven just like dogs or fowls in flight.
"You are kind to ask me.
To complain I'm not free.
In winter of this year
Conscription goes on here.
The magistrates for taxes press.
How can we pay them in distress?
If we had known sons bring no joy,
We would have preferred girl to boy.

生女犹得嫁比邻，
生男埋没随百草。
君不见，
青海头，
古来白骨无人收。
新鬼烦冤旧鬼哭，
天阴雨湿声啾啾。

A daughter can be wed to a neighbor, alas!

A son can only be buried under the grass!"

Have you not seen

On borders green

Bleached bones since olden days unburied on the plain?

The old ghosts weep and cry, while the new ghosts complain;

The air is loud with screech and scream in gloomy rain.

赠李白

秋来相顾尚飘蓬[①]，
未就[②]丹砂[③]愧葛洪。
痛饮狂歌空度日，
飞扬跋扈[④]为谁雄？

① 飘蓬：比喻人的行踪飘忽不定。

② 未就：没有成功。

③ 丹砂：朱砂。

④ 飞扬跋扈（hù）：不守常规，放浪不羁。此处作褒义词用。

《赠李白》是现存杜诗中最早的一首绝句，大约作于公元 745 年李白 45 岁、杜甫 33 岁的时候，所以第一句的“秋来”，既指时间上是秋天，又指李白到了一生中的秋季；“相顾”是说两人都是怀才不遇，同病相怜，所以都像蓬草一样，四处飘零。第二句写诗人不能入世，一展鸿图，只好出世求仙学道，但是冶炼丹砂也无成效，不能像东晋的葛洪一样，炼成丹药升天而去。于是只好痛快地饮酒，狂热地吟诗，几乎是虚度了光阴。什么时候才能像大鹏鸟一样飞腾到九天之上，或者像鲲鱼一样跃起尾巴，翻江倒海，称雄天下呢？这首诗短短四句，写出了两人相知相交的深情厚谊，也写出了诗人放荡不羁、一生寂寞的悲剧。

To Li Bai

When autumn comes, you're drifting still like thistledown;
You try to find the way to heaven, but you fail.
In singing mad and drinking dead your days you drown.
O when will fly the roc? O when will leap the whale?

饮中八仙歌

（节选）

知章骑马似乘船，
眼花落井水底眠。
…………
宗之潇洒美少年，
举觞白眼[①]望青天，
皎如玉树临风[②]前。
…………
李白一斗诗百篇，
长安市上酒家眠，
天子呼来不上船，
自称臣是酒中仙。
张旭三杯草圣传，
脱帽露顶[③]王公前，
挥毫落纸如云烟。

① 白眼：形容看不起的表情。青眼看朋友，白眼视俗人。

② 玉树临风：用玉树来比喻崔宗之的风姿卓越。

③ 脱帽露顶：写张旭狂放不羁的醉态。

《饮中八仙歌》是别具一格、富有特色的“肖像诗”，写的是八位好酒贪饮、飘飘欲仙的诗人。这里只选了四位：第一位是贺知章，他的名作是《回乡偶书》（少小离家老大回）；第二位是崔宗之，就是李白《别友人》（浮云游子意，落日故人情）中的友人；第三位是李白；第四位是书法草

Songs of Eight Immortal Drinkers

(Excerpts)

Zhizhang feels dizzy on his horse as in a boat.
Should he fall in a well, asleep there he would float.

...

Without restraint, Zongzhi is a gallant young guy;
Wine cup in hand, he turns white eyes to the blue sky,
Like one of the jade trees standing in vernal breeze.

...

Li Bai would turn sweet nectar into verses fine.
Drunk in the capital, he'd lie in shops of wine.
Even imperial summons proudly he'd decline,
Saying immortals could not leave the drink divine.
In cursive writing Zhang Xu's worthy of his fame.
After three drinks he bares his head before lord and dame,
And splashes cloud and mist on paper as with flame.

圣张旭，他的名作是《桃花溪》。这里只谈李白，四句诗塑造了一个桀骜不驯、豪放不羁、傲视王侯的艺术形象。尤其是第三句“天子呼来不上船”，使李白的形象显得高大奇伟、神采奕奕，焕发出美的理想光辉，这正是千百年来人民所喜爱的富有浪漫主义色彩的诗人形象。

春日忆李白

白也诗无敌，
飘然思不群[①]。
清新庾开府[②]，
俊逸[③]鲍参军[④]。
渭北春天树，
江东日暮云。
何时一樽酒，
重与细论文[⑤]？

① 不群：不同凡响，胜过同辈。
② 庾（yú）开府：指庾信。
③ 俊逸：形容人貌俊而才高。
④ 鲍参军：指鲍照。
⑤ 论文：论诗。

杜甫与李白在鲁郡东石门分别后，杜甫奔赴长安，公元746或747年杜甫居于长安时作此诗。杜甫在题赠或怀念李白的诗中，总是赞扬备至。此诗中开头四句赞美之热烈，也可看出杜甫对李白非常钦仰。他称赞李白的诗出尘拔俗，清新俊逸，更以古人比之，显示出李白文采的高度。颈联未做任何修饰描绘，看去只是平实的写景，细究之，“渭北”是指诗人所居长安一带，而当时李白正在江东游历，作者将两地景色并列一处，有“碣石潇湘”之意，二人天各一方，牵连着双方的是同样的无限思念。结尾是作者的向往，表达早日重聚的愿望，也是二人惺惺相惜之情的体现。

Thinking of Li Bai on a Spring Day

A poet unequalled by a compeer,
Your fancy flies into celestial sphere.
You freshen up the earth like vernal shower
And beautify the world like brilliant flower.
A towering tree under northern sky,
A floating eastern cloud of sunset dye.
When can we drink together cups of wine
And talk about fine verse and letters fine?

前出塞

（九首其六）

挽[1]弓当挽强，
用箭当用长。
射人先射马，
擒贼先擒王。
杀人亦有限，
列国自有疆[2]。
苟能[3]制侵陵[4]，
岂在多杀伤！

① 挽：拉。
② 疆：边界。
③ 苟能：如果能。
④ 侵陵：侵犯。

据说《前出塞》是写天宝末年哥舒翰征伐吐蕃的事。前四句很像当时军中流行的作战歌诀，讲如何练兵用武，克敌制胜。诗人用了欲擒先纵、先扬后抑的手法。后四句转写战争不应该多杀伤，而要在制止侵略的范围之内，尽量减少伤亡，这样才能体现“止戈为武”的精神。唐诗中以议论为主的很少，这首诗却以议论见长，并且富于哲理。

Song of the Frontier

(VI)

The bow you carry should be strong;
The arrows you use should be long.
Before a horseman, shoot his horse;
Capture the chief to beat his force!
Slaughter shan't go beyond its sphere;
Each State should guard its own frontier.
If an invasion is repelled,
Why shed more blood unless compelled?

丽人行

三月三日天气新，
长安水边多丽人。
态浓意远淑且真[1]，
肌理细腻骨肉匀。
绣罗衣裳照暮春，
蹙金孔雀银麒麟。
头上何所有？
翠微[2]㔩叶[3]垂鬓唇[4]。
背后何所见？
珠压腰衱[5]稳称身。
就中云幕[6]椒房亲[7]，
赐名大国虢与秦。

① 淑且真：形容女子美好而纯真，毫不做作。

② 翠微：薄薄的翡翠片。

③ 㔩（è）叶：一种女子发饰。

④ 鬓唇：鬓边。

⑤ 腰衱（jié）：裙带。

⑥ 云幕：指宫殿中的云状帷幕。

⑦ 椒房亲：指皇后的亲戚。

这首诗约作于公元755年，是讽刺杨贵妃兄妹骄奢荒淫的作品。前十句泛写曲江水边踏青的丽人之众多，仪容之娴雅，体态之优美，衣着之华丽。十一、十二句点明其中有杨家姊妹虢国夫人和秦国夫人。十三至十八句写盛宴的山珍海味。十九至二十二句写宾客盈门。二十三句“杨花雪落覆白苹”，“杨”字暗指杨国忠和虢国夫人的乱伦关系。下一句“青鸟飞去衔红巾”，青鸟是为他们私通传信的使者，红巾却是他们

Satire on Fair Ladies

The weather's fine in the third moon on the third day,
By riverside so many beauties in array.
Each of the ladies has a fascinating face,
Their skin is delicate, their manner full of grace.
Embroidered with peacocks and unicorns in gold,
Their dress in rich silks shines so bright when spring is old.
What do they wear on the head?
Emerald pendant leaves hang down in silver thread.
What do you see from behind?
How nice-fitting are their waistbands with pearls combined.
Among them there're the emperor's favorite kin,
Ennobled Duchess of Guo comes with Duchess of Qin.

幽会的信物。梁启超在《情圣杜甫》中说："如《丽人行》那首七古，全首将近二百字的长篇，完全立在第三者地位观察事实……全首二十六句中之二十四句，只是极力铺叙那种豪奢热闹情状，不仅字面上没有讥刺痕迹，连骨子里头也没有。直至结尾两句：'炙手可热势绝伦，慎莫近前丞相嗔。'算是把主意一逗，但依然不着议论，完全让读者自己去批评，这种可以说是讽刺文学中之最高技术。"

紫驼之峰出翠釜，
水精之盘行素鳞。
犀箸厌饫久未下，
鸾刀缕切空纷纶。
黄门[①]飞鞚不动尘，
御厨络绎送八珍。
箫鼓哀吟感鬼神，
宾从杂遝[②]实要津。
后来鞍马何逡巡，
当轩下马入锦茵。
杨花雪落覆白苹，
青鸟飞去衔红巾。
炙手可热势绝伦，
慎莫近前丞相嗔。

① 黄门：宦官。

② 杂遝（tà）：行人众多，拥挤纷乱。

What do they eat?

The purple meat

Of camel's hump cooked in green cauldron as a dish;

On crystal plate is served snow-white slices of raw fish.

See rhino chopsticks the satiated eaters stay,

And untouched morsels carved by belled knives on the tray.

When eunuchs' horses come running, no dust is raised;

They bring still more rare dishes delicious to the taste.

Listen to soul-stirring music of flutes and drums!

On the main road an official retinue comes.

A rider ambles on saddled horse, the last of all,

He alights, treads on satin carpet, enters the hall.

The willow down like snow falls on the duckweed white;

The blue bird picking red handkerchief goes in flight.

The prime minister's powerful without a peer.

His angry touch would burn your hand. Do not come near!

贫交行

翻手[①]为云覆[②]手雨，
纷纷轻薄[③]何须数[④]。
君不见管鲍[⑤]贫时交，
此道今人弃如土。

① 翻手：比喻人反复无常。

② 覆：颠倒。

③ 轻薄：轻佻，不纯全。

④ 何须数：意谓数不胜数。

⑤ 管鲍：指管仲和鲍叔牙。管仲早年与鲍叔牙相处很好，管仲贫困，也欺骗过鲍叔牙，但鲍叔牙始终善待管仲。现在人们常用“管鲍”来比喻情谊深厚的朋友。

天宝中期，诗人久寓京华，献赋谋职不成，参加科举失利，受尽冷遇，生活困顿之中，饱谙炎凉世态，所以愤而写下此诗。诗开头以翻手覆手、云雨莫测形容世人之交的变化多端，对这种“同利为朋，利尽交疏”的小人之交，诗人给予的是愤慨与蔑视。在黑暗丑陋的现实中，诗人想起了古时的圣贤，而先贤的美德已经被世人随意丢弃，这首短诗是诗人对现实世态的控诉。

Friendship in Poverty

Friends of today are changeable as rain or cloud:

When you are rich or poor, they come and go in crowd.

But a poor man might become a minister wise;

Those looked down upon as dirt to fame may rise.

后出塞

（五首其二）

朝进东门营，
暮上河阳桥。
落日照大旗[①]，
马鸣风萧萧。
平沙列万幕[②]，
部伍各见招。
中天悬明月，
令严夜寂寥。
悲笳[③]数声动，
壮士惨不骄。
借问大将[④]谁？
恐是霍嫖姚[⑤]。

① 大旗：大将用的红旗。

② 幕：帐幕。

③ 悲笳：静营的号令。笳，古代乐器，音色悲壮，常用作军中号角。

④ 大将：指召募统军之将。

⑤ 嫖（piáo）姚（yáo）：同“剽姚”，指霍去病。汉武帝时，霍去病是嫖姚校尉。

后出塞组诗一共五首，这是其中的第二首，以一个刚刚入伍的新兵的口吻，叙述了出征关塞的部伍生活情景。早上进入洛阳城东的军营，晚上到达孟津河阳桥。“落日”四句，描绘了一幅千军万马的壮阔军容，“落日”“平沙”充满了边塞风情。“寂寥”对应前文的“万幕”，又以明月中天衬托“寂寥”，越发映出军令如山下无人作声的安静。这样的寂

Song on the Frontier

(II)

At dawn we come to Camp of Eastern Gate;
At dusk we cross the bridge on Yellow River.
Reddened at sunset, our flags undulate;
In whistling wind our neighing horses quiver.
Thousands of tents aligned on sandy ground,
All the ranks and files answer the roll call.
Bright in the sky above hangs a moon round,
Silence and order reign since the nightfall.
Sad Tartar bugles stir our warriors' heart,
How could they of their homesickness be proud?
What could their commander do for his part,
Even if he could sweep away the cloud?

静中，响起了静营的军号声，一个“悲”字，就写出了悲从中来的意境。至此，这位新兵不禁慨然兴问，统率这支军队的大将是谁呢？但因为时当静营之后，慑于军令的森严，不敢发问，只是心里揣测，大概是像霍去病那样的将领吧！以此结尾，更使军容的壮阔整肃深入人心。

自京赴奉先县咏怀五百字

（节选）

朱门[1]酒肉臭，
路有冻死骨。
荣枯[2]咫尺异，
惆怅[3]难再述。

① 朱门：豪门望族。

② 荣枯：繁荣和落寞。将生活奢靡的豪门与路边冻饿而死的穷人进行对比。

③ 惆怅：感慨，难过。

此诗作于公元 755 年十月，也就是安史之乱爆发的前一个月。诗人在长安久居 10 年，终于得到一个看管兵器铠甲的小官职位。不久诗人由长安往奉先探望妻儿，一路所见，故有此诗。原诗太长，这里只节选了传诵千古的四句。作者通过鲜明的对比，形象地揭示出贫富悬殊的社会现实，诗人忧国忧民的情怀与怀才不遇的现实、山雨欲来的动荡时局、诗人一片赤诚的情感，纷繁复杂地交织成沉郁的诗风，成就了这千古名句。

On the Way from the Capital to Fengxian

(Excerpts)

The mansions burst with wine and meat;

The poor die frozen on the street.

Woe stands within an inch of weal.

Distressed, can I tell what I feel?

月　夜

今夜鄜州[1]月，
闺中[2]只独看。
遥怜[3]小儿女，
未解[4]忆长安。
香雾云鬟湿，
清辉玉臂寒。
何时倚虚幌[5]，
双照泪痕干！

① 鄜（fū）州：今陕西省延安市富县。

② 闺中：指作者的妻子。

③ 怜：疼爱。

④ 未解：不懂。

⑤ 虚幌：薄又透明的帐子。

公元756年六月，安禄山叛军攻进潼关，杜甫携家逃到鄜州羌村。八月杜甫离家，途中被叛军捉住，送到沦陷后的长安，望月思家，写下了这首《月夜》。诗人不说自己思念家人，反说妻子思念自己，可见双方都在思念。“独看”二字，暗示过去曾经同看，更增添了思念之情。说儿女“未解忆长安”，反衬妻子的“忆”，又突出了“独”字；雾湿云

A Moonlit Night

On the moon over Fuzhou which shines bright,
Alone you would gaze in your room tonight.
I'm grieved to think our little children are
Too young to yearn for their father afar.
Your cloudlike hair is moist with dew, it seems;
Your jade-white arms would feel the cold moonbeams.
O when can we stand by the windowside,
Watching the moon with our tear traces dried?

鬟，月寒玉臂，想象妻子望月时间越久，思念越深，不免热泪盈眶，而这眼泪却是最后的“双照泪痕干”泄露出来的。既然双照泪痕才干，独看自然是泪痕不干了。“独看”和“双照”是诗眼，“独看”在诗人是现实，在妻子是想象；“双照”却包括回忆和希望。本诗词旨委婉，章法紧密，所以古人说：“五律至此，无忝诗圣矣！”

悲陈陶[1]

① 陈陶：地名，在长安西北。

孟冬[2]十郡[3]良家子[4]，
血作陈陶泽中水。
野旷天清无战声[5]，
四万义军[6]同日死。
群胡归来血洗箭，
仍唱胡歌饮都市。
都人回面向北啼[7]，
日夜更望官军至。

② 孟冬：农历十月。

③ 十郡（jùn）：指秦中各郡。

④ 良家子：从家世清白的人家中征召的青年士兵。

⑤ 无战声：战事结束，旷野一片安静。

⑥ 义军：所有为国牺牲的士兵。

⑦ 向北啼：唐肃宗驻扎于长安北方的灵武，所以百姓向北而啼。

公元756年冬天，安禄山叛军在长安西北的陈陶泽和唐军作战，唐军义兵四五万人来自西北十郡（今陕西一带），几乎全军覆没，血染陈陶战场，景象惨不忍睹。杜甫当时被困长安，写下了这首纪实诗。第三句“野旷天清无战声”，仿佛天地都在沉痛哀悼牺牲的义士。第五、六句写叛军的骄横得意，衬托出第七、八句人民的悲伤，只有寄希望于官军收复长安了。诗人不只是客观地展现伤痛，而且写出了人民的感情和希望。

Lament on the Defeat at Chentao

In early winter noble sons of household good
Blended with water in Chentao mires their pure blood.
No more war cry beneath the sky on the vast plain;
In one day forty thousand loyal warriors slain.
The enemy came back with blood-stained arrows long;
They drank in market place and shouted barbarous song.
Our countrymen turned north their faces bathed in tears;
Day and night they expect the royal cavaliers.

对　雪

战哭[①]多新鬼[②]，
愁吟[③]独老翁。
乱云低薄暮，
急雪舞回风[④]。
瓢[⑤]弃樽无绿[⑥]，
炉存火似红。
数州消息断，
愁坐[⑦]正书空[⑧]。

① 战哭：在战场上哭泣的士兵。

② 新鬼：死去士兵的亡魂。

③ 愁吟：哀鸣。

④ 回风：旋风。

⑤ 瓢（piáo）：此处指酒葫芦。

⑥ 绿：指酒。

⑦ 愁坐：忧伤地静坐。

⑧ 书空：典出晋代殷浩，用手指在空中虚画字形，形容忧愁或百无聊赖。

这首诗是在长安失陷后写的。安禄山攻陷长安后，诗人逃到半路被叛军抓回。痛苦的心情，艰难的生活，时时折磨着他。房琯所率唐军新败，死伤数万，长安光复无望，又给诗人心头蒙上一层愁苦。诗的开头暗示唐军大败，以及自身所处环境的险恶。三、四两句既点出题目，又对应上文的“独”，身为俘虏，唯有风雪相对，沉郁的困苦愁情被这乱云急雪渲染、放大。诗人的生活也贫困窘迫，酒葫芦在动乱中早已丢弃，酒樽也成了摆设，炉子里仿佛有火在熊熊燃烧，这种想象的手法，把诗人渴望温暖的感受和铁炉的冰冷生动鲜明地展露无遗。末尾回归对家人和局势的担忧，表达了诗人对国家命运的深切关怀。

Facing Snow

So many weep on battlefield;
An old man sings with grief he's filled.
At dusk the tousled clouds fly low;
In swirling wind falls sudden snow.
The gourd and pot not green with wine,
How for a burning stove does he pine!
Could he get news from anywhere?
What can he do but write in air!

春　望

国[1]破山河在，
城春草木深。
感时[2]花溅泪，
恨别鸟惊心。
烽火连三月，
家书抵万金。
白头搔更短[3]，
浑欲不胜簪[4]。

① 国：指都城。
② 感时：感叹时事。
③ 短：少。
④ 不胜簪（zān）：插不上簪子。

《春望》作于公元 757 年三月，安禄山叛军攻陷长安一年之后。诗一开始就写国都沦陷，城池残破，虽然山河依旧，可是乱草遍地，林木苍苍，已经人事全非了。这表面上是写景，实际上是抒情。接着诗人有感于时世艰难，看见美丽的花朵反而会流泪；因恨家破人散，听见欢乐

Spring View

On war-torn land streams flow and mountains stand;
In vernal town grass and weeds are o'ergrown.
Grieved o'er the years, flowers make us shed tears;
Hating to part, hearing birds breaks our heart.
The beacon fire has gone higher and higher;
Words from household are worth their weight in gold.
I cannot bear to scratch my grizzling hair;
It grows too thin to hold a light hairpin.

的鸟叫也会胆战心惊。战争已经从去年三月打到今年三月，得到一封家信都抵得上万两黄金。诗人担惊受怕，头发都变白了，急得直搔头，而头发越搔越少，少得连发簪都插不住了。这首诗寄情于物，托感于景，情景交融，表达了诗人爱国爱家的一片真心，是传诵千年的名诗。

哀江头

少陵野老吞声哭[1]，
春日潜行[2]曲江曲。
江头宫殿锁千门，
细柳新蒲为谁绿[3]？
忆昔霓旌[4]下南苑，
苑中万物生颜色[5]。
昭阳殿里第一人，
同辇随君侍君侧。
辇前才人带弓箭，
白马嚼啮黄金勒。
翻身向天仰射云[6]，
一笑正坠双飞翼。

① 吞声哭：不敢出声地哭泣。
② 潜行：偷偷地走到这里。
③ 为谁绿：国破家亡，连草木都失去了故人。
④ 霓（ní）旌：指天子的旗。
⑤ 生颜色：蓬勃生辉。
⑥ 仰射云：仰射云间飞过的鸟。

《哀江头》也是公元757年春天的作品。江指曲江，在长安的东南。汉武帝在江边修建了亭台楼阁，是汉唐两代的游览名胜。但安禄山攻占长安之后，宫门上锁，庭苑荒芜。杜甫一人偷偷前来，抚今追昔，不禁感慨系之，就写下了这首《哀江头》。前四句写沦陷后曲折多致的曲江已经人物全非，今非昔比了。自第五句起，八句回忆沦陷前春到曲江的繁华景象，特写唐玄宗和杨贵妃同车来游，宫中女官戎装侍卫，一箭射

Lament along the Winding River

Old and deprived, I swallow tears on a spring day;
Along Winding River in stealth I go my way.
All palace gates and doors are locked on rivershore;
Willows and reeds are green for no one to adore.
I remember rainbow banners streamed at high tide
To Southern Park where everything was beautified.
The first lady of the Sunny Palace would ride
In the imperial chariot by the emperor's side.
The horsewomen before her bore arrows and bow;
Their white steeds champed at golden bits on the front row.
One archer, leaning back, shot at cloud in the sky;
One arrow brought down two winged birds from on high.

下两只大雁的盛况。自第十三句起，写杨贵妃因兵变惨死马嵬坡，身为游魂，欲归不得，而唐玄宗却经由剑阁入川，生死隔绝了。最后四句诗人见景伤情，感慨深沉，用无情的江水江花来反衬，更显得诗人情深。这深情表现在行动上，就是他本来要回城南，却心烦意乱，反而走向城北了。诗人在表达爱国热忱之时，也流露了对君王的伤悼之情。

明眸皓齿今何在?
血污游魂归不得。
清渭东流剑阁深,
去住彼此无消息。
人生有情泪沾臆,
江水江花岂终极?
黄昏胡骑①尘满城,
欲往城南望城北。

① 胡骑:指叛军的骑兵。

Where are the first lady's pearly teeth and eyes bright?

Her spirit, blood-stained, could not come back from the height.

Far from Sword Cliff, with River Wei her soul flew east;

The emperor got no news from her in the least.

A man who has a heart will wet his breast with tears.

Would riverside grass and flowers not weep for years?

At dusk the rebels' horses overrun the town;

I want to go upward, but instead I go down.

喜达行在所

（三首其二）

愁思胡笳夕，
凄凉汉苑[①]春。
生还今日事，
间道[②]暂时人。
司隶[③]章初睹，
南阳气已新。
喜心翻倒极，
呜咽泪沾巾。

① 汉苑：此处以汉代比唐代，如曲江、南苑等地。

② 间道：易于逃窜的小道。

③ 司隶：代指朝廷官员。

行在所，指朝廷临时政府所在地。公元757年四月，杜甫冒险逃出被叛军占据的长安，投奔在凤翔的唐肃宗。历尽千辛万苦，他终于到达了目的地。当年五月，唐肃宗拜杜甫为左拾遗。《喜达行在所》是组诗，这是其中第二首。开篇追忆当年身陷叛军时，夜闻胡笳则愁，春回旧苑则悲。汉苑实指唐宫，旧日宫墙记录着往日的繁华，似诉今日凄凉。诗

At the Temporary Imperial Court

(II)

Sad to hear the Tartar bugle at nightfall
And see the royal garden desolate,
How glad I'm now to answer royal call
After living as a captive of late!
I'm happy to assume an office new
When the imperial court will thrive again,
But memory of the past comes in view,
Tears stream down and leave on my sleeves their stain.

人刚刚生还，惊魂未定，不久之前，逃亡途中的事还历历在目，仿佛仍然随时都会死去，故称“暂时人”。“司隶”两句描写朝廷新气象，借用刘秀光武中兴重整汉室的典故，南阳是刘秀的故乡，刘秀拨乱反正，正如今日凤翔景象。眼见中兴有望，诗人喜极而泣。

羌　村

（三首其一）

峥嵘[1]赤云西[2]，
日脚下平地。
柴门鸟雀噪，
归客千里至。
妻孥[3]怪我在，
惊定还拭泪。
世乱遭飘荡，
生还偶然遂[4]！
邻人满墙头，
感叹亦歔欷[5]。
夜阑[6]更秉烛，
相对如梦寐。

① 峥嵘：形容山峰高峻。

② 赤云西：赤云的西边。

③ 妻孥（nú）：妻子和儿女。

④ 遂：如愿以偿。

⑤ 歔（xū）欷（xī）：悲泣之声。

⑥ 夜阑：深夜。

公元 757 年秋天，杜甫回到羌村，全家久别重逢，悲喜交集，诗人写了三首《羌村》，这里选的是第一首。前四句写夕阳西下时，杜甫到羌村的情况。诗人把璀璨的晚霞比作峥嵘的山峰，把云缝中照射下来的光线叫作“日脚”，仿佛太阳经过了一天的奔波，急于西下，正如诗人经过了长途跋涉，急于回家一样，这又是情景交融了。鸟雀的叫声反衬

Coming Back to Qiang Village

(I)

Like rugged hills hangs gilt-edged cloud;
The sunset sheds departing ray.
The wicket gate with birds is loud
When I come back from far away.
At my appearance starts my wife;
Then calming down, she melts in tears.
By chance I come back still in life,
While people drift in bitter years.
My neighbors look over the wall;
They sigh and from their eyes tears stream.
When night comes, candles light the hall;
We sit face to face as in dream.

出了山村的荒凉萧条。中间四句写妻子见面不敢相信，不敢相认，甚至发愣了；这刻画出了患难余生的心理状态。后四句先写邻人围观，寥寥十字，富有人情味。后写家人深夜烛下对坐，反疑相见是梦，真是入木三分。全诗用白描手法，取材于一时见闻，景实情真，写出了典型的生活情景和人物的心理活动，所以读来耐人寻味。

曲　江[1]

（二首其一）

① 曲江：唐代地名，位于今陕西西安东南郊的河流，游玩佳处。

一片花飞减却春[2]，
风飘万点[3]正愁人。
且看欲尽花经眼，
莫厌伤多酒入唇。
江上小堂巢翡翠[4]，
苑边高冢[5]卧麒麟。
细推[6]物理[7]须行乐，
何用浮名[8]绊此身？

② 减却春：减少春色。

③ 万点：很多的落花。

④ 巢翡翠：翡翠鸟筑巢。

⑤ 冢（zhǒng）：坟墓。

⑥ 推：推究。

⑦ 物理：事物的道理。

⑧ 浮名：虚名。

这首诗作于公元 758 年暮春，唐军已收复长安，安史之乱渐渐平息，但这场浩劫留下的是满目疮痍。回到长安后，宦官李辅国擅权，左拾遗杜甫受到排挤，心情极度烦闷，于是借此诗伤春感时。开篇语奇而意境深远，终于盼到春暖花开，而春光易逝花易老，转眼已是残春景象。每落一片花瓣，都会减掉一丝春色，何况“风飘万点”，怎不使人伤春惜春。颔联写花飞欲尽，莫不经眼，作者借酒浇愁，无心去想酒多伤身。颈联

The Winding River

(I)

Each fallen petal means a bit of spring passed away.
How sad to see so many blown down by the breeze!
Before all blossoms fall by the end of the day,
Fear not to drink more wine would put your mind at ease!
Kingfishers build their nest in a riverside hall;
An unicorn in stone before the graveyard lies.
We should enjoy life in response to nature's call.
Why should we seek for vainglory in people's eyes?

写曲江的荒凉颓废，江上的小堂，因长期无人，小鸟巢其中；苑边的陵墓，久无人祭扫，墓饰倒卧杂草。经过一番动荡，繁华不再，昔日盛况难返，寄寓作者对世事无常的感慨。然而道法自然，万物兴废本是自然之理，宇宙万物之间，所有荣华兴盛都只是昙花一现，又何必为浮名所累，还是快意人生及时行乐吧。

曲　江

（二首其二）

朝回[①]日日典[②]春衣，
每日江头尽醉归。
酒债寻常行处[③]有，
人生七十古来稀。
穿花蛱蝶深深[④]见[⑤]，
点水蜻蜓款款飞。
传语风光共流转[⑥]，
暂时相赏莫相违[⑦]。

①朝回：下朝回来。
②典：典当。
③行处：所到之处。
④深深：在花丛深处。
⑤见：通“现”。
⑥共流转：在一起逗留、徘徊。
⑦违：错过。

暮春时节，诗人下朝回来，典当春衣买醉，生活清贫如此。典当春衣，有可能是因为冬衣已经当完，终日醺醺，可见其仕不得志。典衣买酒终是杯水车薪，故处处赊有酒债，诗人对此的评论是“人生七十古来稀”，人生苦短，既然仕途不得志，姑且“莫思身外无穷事，且尽生前有限杯”。“穿花”两句是杜诗中的名句，这一联不事雕琢，有璞玉天成之妙，“深深”映照出“穿”的灵巧，“款款”衬托出“点”的优雅，这两句对仗工整，意境恬然自得。美好的事物总是短暂的，恰如短暂的人生，所以风光如许，不可辜负，诗人于无奈的尘世中，寻得一丝慰藉。

The Winding River

(II)

I pawn my spring gown after audience day by day,
To drink my fill in riverside shops all the way.
No wonder there's no shop but I owe debt of wine.
If not, why live to seventy like an old pine?
Butterflies gather honey from flower to flower;
Dragonflies skim over water lower and lower.
Let us enjoy more wine with ease as time evolves!
Do not regret too late when sun or moon revolves!

曲江对酒

苑[1]外江头坐不归，
水精宫殿[2]转霏微[3]。
桃花细逐杨花落，
黄鸟时兼白鸟飞。
纵饮久判[4]人共弃，
懒朝真与世相违。
吏情更觉沧洲[5]远，
老大徒伤未拂衣[6]。

① 苑：曲江西南的芙蓉苑，是帝妃游玩的地方。

② 水精宫殿：指芙蓉苑中的宫殿。

③ 霏微：迷濛的样子。

④ 判（pān）：甘愿。

⑤ 沧洲：指隐士的居处。

⑥ 拂衣：拂袖而去，告老还乡。

这首诗写于公元758年，杜甫最后留居长安时。诗一开首就说坐在江头不愿归去，说明已久坐多时，可见诗人心中情绪，为下文做铺垫。第二句表意是写薄暮之下，墙垣宫殿一片朦胧，实则是说昔时风光今已不再，时过境迁，盛衰在目，仿佛一切如昨，转眼便归于尘土。作为一同目睹过繁华成空而又被忘却的见证者，诗人就想这样守着这一江春水，守着这断井残垣，看着桃花追逐杨花争相落下，看着黄鹂白鹭竞相飞走，看着它们纷纷离去，而诗人自认纵酒多时已被厌弃，也不愿违心做出勤谨政事的虚伪表象，如果不是微职在身年纪又大，诗人也想离开，找一处水边，或就在这苑外江头，终日闲坐。这首诗寄情于景物花鸟，反映出诗人理想成空，报国无门的苦楚。

Drinking by Poolside

I won't come back, sitting by poolside ill at ease,
Till crystal palaces turn dim and low in twilight.
Peach blossoms fall with willow-down blown by the breeze,
When yellow birds spread wings with white birds in their flight.
Seeking no favor, I drink my wine all the day;
I'm not assiduous in the court where I feel cold.
Longing in office for my hermitage far away,
Why do I not resign before I grow too old?

九日蓝田[1]崔氏庄

① 蓝田：今陕西省西安市蓝田县。

老去悲秋强[2]自宽，
兴来今日尽君欢。
羞将短发还吹帽，
笑倩[3]旁人为正冠。
蓝水[4]远从千涧落，
玉山[5]高并两峰寒。
明年此会知谁健[6]？
醉把茱萸仔细看。

② 强：勉强。

③ 倩：请。

④ 蓝水：蓝田山下的蓝溪。

⑤ 玉山：蓝田山。

⑥ 健：在。

诗人感到自己已经并且仍在老去，面对寂寥秋景更是悲由心生，只得勉强宽慰自己。所以重阳这天，一定要和友人尽欢而散。前两句犹如题记，交代了此诗的创作时间和背景，其意辗转曲折，诗句婉转自如。颔联借用"孟嘉落帽"的典故，倾诉自己有心向往前人的风流蕴藉，怎奈如今地位尴尬，只得"笑倩旁人为正冠"，虽笑犹悲，悲凉之情深刻入骨。颈联笔锋一转，描山绘水，气象峥嵘，意高而境远，豪迈苍凉，力透纸背。明年此际，山水固然如故，然而人事终难料，那时又有几人健在呢？结尾不置一言，只将寄托对亲朋好友的相思之情的茱萸细看，饱含诗人无法释怀的满腹忧愁。

Mountain-climbing Day in Blue Field

How to console an old man on an autumn day?
High mountains bring high spirit, I'm happy and gay.
My hat blown down reveals my short hair, I feel shy;
Smiling, I ask you to put it right with a sigh.
Blue water comes from a thousand creeks far away;
Jade Mountain stands with two high peaks cold cloud to stay.
After we part, can we meet here again next year?
Drunken, I ask dogwood if it will reappear.

日　暮

牛羊下来久，
各已闭柴门。
风月自清夜，
江山非故园[①]。
石泉流暗壁[②]，
草露滴秋根[③]。
头白灯明里，
何须花烬[④]繁？

① 故园：故乡。

② 石泉流暗壁：就是“暗泉流石壁”。

③ 草露滴秋根：就是“秋露滴草根”。秋根，秋天的草根。

④ 花烬：灯芯燃烧后结成的像花一样的物体，民间常以此为喜兆。

公元767年秋，诗人在流寓夔州瀼西东屯期间，写下了这首诗。余晖遍洒的宁静山村，牛羊早已从山野之中归来，家家户户柴扉紧闭，一片阒然幽静中，使人想起户内人们享受天伦之乐的情景。皓月明空，照着寂静的村庄，也照着诗人孤单的身影。诗人看着这明丽如画的风景，怎奈这不是故乡，于是思乡的愁肠被触动。颈联有意把“暗泉流石壁，秋露滴草根”错置词序，使诗句更为铿锵顿挫，使诗意更为奇逸浓郁。

After Nightfall

Long have cattle come to the pen,
And closed are all wicker gates then.
Beautiful is the moonlit night,
But my homeland is not in sight.
Water flows from fountains unseen;
Dewdrops drip on autumn grass green.
My white hair twinkling by lamplight,
Do I need flowers gleaming bright?

清新洁净的意境下，凄寂幽邃的夜景中，带给人一丝悲凉、抑郁之感。结尾仿佛是一声叹息，诗人已是迟暮之年，白发与灯光交相辉映，仕途一无所成，归乡又遥遥无期，饱尝生活的辛酸，因而面对似在报喜的灯花，不但不觉欢欣，反而备感烦恼，仿佛喜兆和自己根本无缘，婉转曲折，耐人寻味。

独　立

空外[1]一鸷鸟[2]，
河间双白鸥[3]。
飘飖[4]搏击便，
容易往来游。
草露亦多湿，
蛛丝仍未收。
天机近人事，
独立万端忧。

① 空外：虚空之外。

② 鸷鸟：比喻小人。

③ 白鸥：比喻君子。

④ 飘飖（yáo）：形容轻盈洒脱的样子。

《独立》读来像一首寓言诗。第一联说：天上一只鹰，河中两只鸥。对仗工整。第二联说：鹰从天上冲下来，白鸥却还无忧无虑，从容不迫，在河中游来游去。这两句形式相对，意义相反。第三联说草上的露水会沾湿飞虫的翅膀，蜘蛛的罗网会捕捉小虫，所以小虫和白鸥一样，都在危险之中，却无警惕之心。第四联就把天人结合起来，说天上人间一样危险，诗人独立无言，不禁忧从中来。

Alone I Stand

A falcon hovers in the sky;
A pair of gulls on water glide.
The falcon darts down from on high
On gulls floating on river wide.
The dewy grass may wet the wing;
The spider's net may trap the weak.
Nature and man are the same thing.
Aggrieved alone, I cannot speak.

赠卫八处士

人生不相见，
动如参与商。
今夕复何夕？
共此灯烛光。
少壮能几时？
鬓发各已苍[①]。
访旧半为鬼，
惊呼热中肠。
焉知二十载，
重上君子堂？
昔别君未婚，
儿女忽成行。

① 苍：灰白色。

《唐史拾遗》中说：“杜甫与李白、高适、卫宾相友善，时宾年最小，号小友。”卫八处士可能就是卫宾，八是排行，处士就是不出仕的隐士。这首诗是公元759年写的。前十句抒情，先说会面之难，可见相会之乐。中间转为叙事，说到变化之大，儿女成长之快，主人款待之殷，写出了朋友之情，长幼之义。最后两句想到明天的别离，今天的相会越乐，明天的离别就越悲。全诗前后一片茫茫，更显得诗意沉郁了。

For Wei the Eighth

How rarely together friends are!
As Morning Star with Evening Star.
O what a rare night is tonight?
Together we share candlelight.
How long can last our youthful years?
Grey hair on our temples appears.
We find half of our friends departed.
How can we not cry broken-hearted!
After twenty years, who knows then,
I come into your hall again.
Unmarried twenty years ago,
Now you have children in a row.

怡然敬父执[1]，
问我来何方？
问答乃未已[2]，
儿女罗酒浆。
夜雨剪春韭，
新炊[3]间黄粱[4]。
主称会面难，
一举累[5]十觞。
十觞亦不醉，
感子故意长[6]。
明日隔山岳，
世事两茫茫。

① 父执：父亲经常接近的朋友。

② 乃未已：话未说完。

③ 新炊：刚煮好的新鲜饭。

④ 黄粱：黄米。

⑤ 累：连续。

⑥ 故意长：老友间的深情厚谊。

Seeing their father's friend at home,
They're glad to ask where I come from.
Our talk has not come to an end,
When wine is offered to the friend.
They bring leeks cut after night rain
And millet cooked with new grain.
The host says, "It is hard to meet.
Let us drink ten cups of wine sweet!"
Ten cupfuls cannot make me drunk,
For deep in your love I am sunk.
Mountains will divide us tomorrow.
O What can we foresee but sorrow!

新安吏

客行新安道，

喧呼闻点兵。

借问新安吏：

“县小更[①]无丁？”

“府帖昨夜下，

次[②]选中男行。”

“中男[③]绝短小，

何以守王城？”

肥男有母送，

瘦男独伶俜[④]。

白水暮东流，

青山犹哭声。

① 更：难道。

② 次：依次。

③ 中男：指十八岁以上、二十三岁以下的成丁。

④ 伶俜（pīng）：形容孤独。

公元758年，郭子仪打败了叛军，收复了长安和洛阳，但得不到唐肃宗的信任，军粮不足，士气低落，反在邺城打了败仗。唐王朝为了补充兵力，大肆抽丁拉夫。杜甫这时经过洛阳以西的新安，耳闻目睹了这次惨败后人民所遭受的痛苦，写下了“三吏”“三别”六篇史诗。《新安吏》写的是征兵本来应该征21岁以上的壮丁，但是壮丁不足，只好抓十几

A Recruiting Sergeant at Xin'an

I pass by Xin'an on my way
And hear sergeants call roll and bray.
I ask one of this county small
If he can draft adults at all.
Last night came order for hands green,
Draft age is lowered to eighteen.
The teenagers are small and short.
How can they hold the royal fort?
Fat sons still need their mothers' care;
Weak ones look lonely in despair.
At dusk the pale stream flows east still;
Their wails echo from hill to hill.

岁的中男。中男抓走之后，哭声仍然在耳，仿佛连青山白水也在呜咽一样，这就是诗人移情于景了。杜甫同情壮丁，但又不能怨恨王朝。于是只好安慰壮丁说：战壕不会挖得太深，放马的劳役也不会太重，加上郭子仪将军对士兵情若父兄，所以放心去当兵吧。本诗既反映了壮丁的悲苦，又流露了诗人的用心。这就是杜甫的现实主义了。

“莫自使眼枯，
收汝泪纵横。
眼枯即见骨，
天地终无情。
我军取相州，
日夕望其平。
岂意贼难料，
归军星散营。
就粮近故垒，
练卒依旧京。
掘壕不到水，
牧马役亦轻。
况乃王师顺，
抚养甚分明。
送行勿泣血，
仆射①如父兄。”

① 仆射：指郭子仪。

Don't cry until your eyes go dry!
Let no tears crisscross your face wry!
Though to skin and bone your eyes go,
No mercy would the Heaven show.
Our force should take Xiangzhou with might,
Victory expected day and night.
But rebels not easy to beat
Counter-attack, our troops retreat.
We've grain enough in our stronghold,
And training camp near capital old.
To dig deep trench you do not need;
It is not hard to tend the steed.
The royal force has at its head
General Guo by whom you're well fed.
Don't shed at parting bloody tears!
The general treats you as compeers.

石壕吏

暮投石壕村，
有吏[①]夜捉人。
老翁逾[②]墙走，
老妇出门看。
吏呼一何怒！
妇啼一何苦！
听妇前致词：
“三男邺城戍[③]。
一男附书至，
二男新战死。
存者且偷生，
死者长已矣！

① 吏：指来抓壮丁的低级官吏。

② 逾（yú）：越过，翻过。

③ 戍（shù）：驻守，指服役。

《石壕吏》是“三吏”中最著名的一篇，全篇重点在“有吏夜捉人”一句。《新安吏》中还是征兵，《石壕吏》中却是捉人，可见情况更加严重。诗中说道：三男戍，二男死，孙方幼，媳无裙，翁逾墙，妇夜往。抓壮丁抓不到，连老妇人都拉去当差，可见民不聊生。全诗非常简练，在“吏呼一何怒”之后，不再写吏，而只写妇致词，这用的是寓问于答的写法。古人评说：“其事何长！其言何简！”全篇句句叙事，没有抒

The Pressgang at Stone Moat Village

I seek for shelter at nightfall.
What is the pressgang coming for?
My old host climbs over the wall;
My old hostess answers the door.
How angry is the sergeant's shout!
How bitter is the woman's cry!
I hear what she tries to speak out.
"I'd three sons guarding the town high.
One wrote a letter telling me
That his brothers were killed in war.
He'll keep alive if he can be;
The dead have passed and are no more.

情，没有议论，但是通过叙事，却流露出了诗人的爱憎之情、褒贬之意。梁启超在《情圣杜甫》中谈到"三吏"时说："这些诗是要作者的精神和那所写之人的精神并合为一，才能作出。……作这首《石壕吏》时，他已经化身做那位儿女死绝衣食不给的老太婆，所以他说的话，完全和他们自己说一样。……这类诗的好处在真，事愈写得详，真情愈发得透，我们熟读他，可以理会得'真即是美'的道理。"

室中更无人，
惟有乳下孙。
有孙母未去[①]，
出入无完裙。
老妪力虽衰，
请从吏夜归。
急应河阳役，
犹得备晨炊。”
夜久语声绝，
如闻泣幽咽[②]。
天明登前途[③]，
独与老翁别。

① 去：离开，这里指改嫁。

② 泣幽咽：低声细小断续的哭声。

③ 登前途：上路。

In the house there is no man left,
Except my grandson in the breast
Of his mother, of all bereft;
She can't come out, in tatters dressed.
Though I'm a woman weak and old,
I beg to go tonight with you,
That I may serve in the stronghold
And cook morning meals as my due."
With night her voices fade away;
I seem to hear still sob and sigh.
At dawn again I go my way
And only bid my host goodbye.

潼关[1]吏

① 潼关：地名，位于华州华阴县东北，今陕西省渭南市潼关县北。

士卒何草草，
筑城潼关道。
大城铁不如，
小城万丈余。
借问潼关吏：
“修关还备胡[2]？”
要[3]我下马行，
为我指山隅：
“连云列战格，
飞鸟不能逾。
胡来但自守，
岂复忧西都[4]。

② 备胡：抵御安史叛军。

③ 要：同“邀”，邀请。

④ 西都：指长安。

唐军在邺城战败后，恐怕洛阳失守，又在潼关修筑工事。杜甫经过时，向潼关吏了解情况。问答中穿插了叙事和议论，这和《新安吏》《石壕吏》不同。《潼关吏》前四句是总写，“草草”是辛苦的意思。杜甫问后，没有立刻写关吏的回答，而是插了两句叙事，然后才描写关山险阻，请杜甫老丈放心，只要一夫当关，就可以万夫莫开。关吏的话使诗人想

Officer at the Western Pass

How hard do soldiers work and toil,
Building ramparts on western soil!
Iron-clad bastions high and low
Like walls along the mountain go.
I ask an officer near by
If against foes are built walls high.
He asks me to dismount and look
Around and points to mountain nook.
The forts on the peaks scrape the sky,
Over them even birds can't fly.
When come the foe, we guard the wall,
There's no fear for the capital.

起了桃林之败，于是发了几句议论。原来三年前叛军进攻潼关，守将哥舒翰要坚守，但宰相杨国忠促战，哥舒翰不得不出关迎敌，在灵宝以西的桃林塞大战，结果全军覆没，很多士兵葬身鱼腹。杜甫听了关吏自信的话，发了一番感慨，要守将谨慎从事，不能再蹈哥舒翰的覆辙。从诗中可以看出杜甫忠君爱国爱民之心。

丈人[1]视要处，

窄狭容单车。

艰难奋[2]长戟，

万古用一夫。”

“哀哉桃林[3]战，

百万化为鱼。

请嘱防关将，

慎勿学哥舒！”

① 丈人：关吏对杜甫的尊称。

② 奋：挥动。

③ 桃林：桃林塞，指河南省灵宝市以西至潼关一带的地方。

He shows me the narrow pass too,
Only single chariots file through.
When guarded with long spear by one,
The fortress can be forced by none.
But defeated at Peach Grove, alas!
Ten thousand men slain at the pass.
Please tell the general guarding here:
Be not defeated as that year!

新婚别

兔丝[1]附蓬麻，
引蔓故不长。
嫁女与征夫，
不如弃路旁。
结发为妻子，
席不暖君床。
暮婚晨告别，
无乃太匆忙！
君行虽不远，
守边赴河阳[2]。
妾身未分明，
何以拜姑嫜[3]？
父母养我时，
日夜令我藏。

① 兔丝：植物名，又名无根草。一种依附于其他植物生长的寄生植物。

② 河阳：唐军与叛军对峙之处。

③ 姑嫜（zhāng）：公婆。

“三吏”主要是用问答方式写的，诗中有诗人和官吏的对话，或老妇对官吏的回答。“三别”却是用独白方式写的，诗中没有诗人出现，如《新婚别》就是新娘内心的独白。开始写新娘诉说自己不幸的命运，内容非常有戏剧性，却以比喻开始，把自己比作蔓草，缠绕在蓬麻上，注定了生长不长的。所以昨夜洞房花烛，今晨就要生离死别。而根据古代婚礼，三天以后才能拜见公婆，这

Lament of the Newly Wed

The creeper clinging to the flax is wrong,
For it can't be expected to grow long.
If a maiden to a soldier is tied
In wedlock, better forsake her by roadside.
My hair dressed up, to you I'm newly wed,
But we have not yet warmed our nuptial bed.
Married last night, at dawn we bid adieu.
Why should I part in such hurry with you?
Though you may not be very far away,
Only in Heyang garrison you'll stay.
I have not performed the rites of a wife.
How can I serve your parents all my life?
Bred by my parents, I was told it's right
To hide indoors every day and night.

样一夜夫妻，连身份都不明呢。接着新娘把话题由自身转到丈夫身上，说自己嫁鸡随鸡，而丈夫要上战场，自己又不能跟随，只能待在家里，心乱如麻。再后写新娘以理化情，鼓励丈夫从军，自己宁可不穿罗衣，不施脂粉，在家等候丈夫回来。最后又以比喻作结，看见百鸟双飞，觉得自己反而不如鸟了。这首诗写出了新娘矛盾曲折的心理，从中可以看出诗人同情人民、反对战争的思想。

生女有所归[1]，
鸡狗亦得将。
君今往死地，
沉痛迫中肠。
誓欲随君去，
形势反苍黄[2]。
勿为新婚念，
努力事戎行。
妇人在军中，
兵气恐不扬。
自嗟贫家女，
久致罗襦裳[3]。
罗襦不复施，
对君洗红妆。
仰视百鸟飞，
大小必双翔[4]。
人事多错迕，
与君永相望。

① 归：出嫁。

② 苍黄：同“仓皇”，形容慌张失措的样子。这里指会带来麻烦。

③ 襦裳：襦为短衣，裳为下衣。

④ 双翔：成双成对地飞翔。

Oh, I am destined to go to your house
Like a hen or a dog to be your spouse.
Now you go to a place in face of death,
How can I not utter my painful breath?
I would follow you wherever you go,
But I fear it would bring less weal than woe.
So forget the bride in your family then,
But do your duty as all army men.
If there were women in the camp, I fear,
It's no good for morale on the frontier.
As a daughter of a poor family,
It's difficult to get silk robe for me.
But I fear I could not wear it again,
Rougeless and powderless I would remain.
Looking up, I see hundreds of birds fly,
Big or small, all of them in pairs on high.
Why different should be our human fate?
O how long, how long should I for you wait!

垂老别

四郊未宁静，
垂老不得安。
子孙阵亡尽，
焉用身独完[①]！
投杖出门去，
同行为辛酸。
幸有牙齿存，
所悲骨髓干[②]。
男儿既介胄[③]，
长揖别上官。
老妻卧路啼，
岁暮衣裳单。
孰知是死别，
且复伤其寒。

① 身独完：独自活下去。

② 骨髓干：形容身体的衰老。

③ 介胄：即“甲胄”，指铠甲、头盔。

《石壕吏》写“有吏夜捉人”，捉走的是老妇；《垂老别》写官府征兵，征去的却是老翁。这首叙事诗不以情节曲折取胜，而以人物的心理刻画见长。诗人用老翁的自诉自叹，对人对己的安慰语气来展开描写，着重表现人物时而沉重忧愤，时而自作旷达的复杂心理。杜甫高于一般诗人的地方，主要在于他无论是叙事还是抒情，都能做到立足生活，深入人心，通过个

Lament of an Old Man

In all the country there's no peace.
How can an old man live with ease?
Sons and grandsons in battle slain,
Why should my old body remain?
Casting my staff away, I go;
My companions compassion show.
Fortunately my teeth are sound,
But in my bones no marrow's found.
As soldier clad in armor now,
To officers I make a bow.
By the roadside cries my wife old,
So thinly clad in winter cold.
Who knows if we can meet again?
Seeing her shiver, I feel pain.

别反映一般，准确传神地表现他那个时代的生活现实，概括劳动人民的辛酸苦难。诗中老翁担心老妻受寒着凉，老妻劝老翁要努力加餐，这些生活中极其寻常的劝慰语言，出现在极不寻常的生离死别的背景之下，便收到了惊心动魄的艺术效果。有时老翁故作旷达之语，但也不能掩饰内心的矛盾，反倒流露出了乱世的真情。这就是杜诗为什么被称为“诗史”的原因。

此去必不归，
还闻劝加餐。
土门[1]壁甚坚，
杏园[2]度亦难。
势异邺城下，
纵死时犹宽。
人生有离合，
岂择衰盛[3]端[4]！
忆昔少壮日，
迟回竟长叹。
万国尽征戍，
烽火被冈峦[5]。
积尸草木腥，
流血川原丹。
何乡为乐土？
安敢尚盘桓！
弃绝蓬室居，
塌然摧肺肝[6]。

① 土门：土门关。唐代防守的要地。

② 杏园：唐军防守的要地，位于今河南省卫辉市东南。

③ 衰盛：一作“衰老”。

④ 端：思绪。

⑤ 被冈峦：遍布整个山冈。

⑥ 摧肺肝：极度悲痛的样子。

Once gone, I can't come back, I fear;
She still says, "Eat more!" to my ear.
I tell her the fortress is strong,
To cross the stream takes a time long.
Unlike the siege of days gone by,
It's not so soon for me to die.
To meet or part is fate in life,
Whether with a young or old wife.
Remembering when I was strong,
Can I not heave sighs deep and long!
War's raging in the countryside;
Beacon fire blazes far and wide.
Grass and trees stink with bodies dead;
With blood the streams and plains turn red.
Where can I find a happy land?
Why do I tarry here and stand?
Why not from my humble home part
And march away with broken heart!

无家别

寂寞天宝后[①]，
园庐[②]但蒿藜。
我里百余家，
世乱各东西。
存者无消息，
死者为尘泥。
贱子因阵败，
归来寻旧蹊。
久行见空巷，
日瘦[③]气惨凄。
但对狐与狸，
竖毛怒我啼。
四邻何所有?
一二老寡妻。

① 天宝后：安史之乱后。安史之乱爆发于天宝年间，故称“天宝后”。

② 庐：住所，房屋。

③ 日瘦：日光淡薄。

“三别”中《新婚别》写的是年轻的新婚夫妇，《垂老别》写的是年高的老夫老妻，《无家别》写的却是无家可归的中年男子。无家可归的人自称“贱子”，在战乱后回到家乡，只见一片荒凉，满目蒿藜。昔日百户人家，今日只见空巷。天上的太阳也愁容满面，消瘦暗淡；地上不见人迹，只有狐狸出没。近景描写细致，刻画入微。空宅凄凄，家人早

Lament of a Homeless

Since the rebellion I feel lone,
My house with weeds is overgrown.
A hundred homes can find no rest;
People are scattered east and west.
None knows where the living have fled,
While to dust have returned the dead.
My humble self after the defeat
Come back to find my old retreat.
I walk long on deserted lanes.
The sun grows lean where drear air reigns.
In face of bristling fox or cat,
I am afraid to be growled at.
How many neighbors left, all told?
Only one or two widows old.

已故去，抚今忆昔，不禁感慨系之，把自己比作无枝可栖的归鸟。不料县吏知道他回来了，又征调他去打鼓。于是他自喜自伤，喜的是在本州服役，伤的是无人送别；但一想到还要远去打仗，远近又有什么分别？这样层层深入地分析他的心理变化，又通过环境的描写，反映人物的思想感情。

宿鸟恋本枝，
安辞且穷栖。
方春独荷锄，
日暮还灌畦。
县吏知我至，
召令习鼓鞞。
虽从本州役，
内顾无所携[1]。
近行止一身，
远去终转迷[2]。
家乡既荡尽，
远近理亦齐。
永痛长病母，
五年委沟溪[3]。
生我不得力，
终身两酸嘶[4]。
人生无家别，
何以为蒸黎[5]！

① 无所携：家里没有人可以作别。

② 终转迷：终究前途未卜，生死难料。

③ 委沟溪：母亲被埋葬在山谷中。

④ 酸嘶：指哀鸣悲叹。

⑤ 蒸黎：劳动人民。

A bird will not leave its own nest,
My house, though poor, will give me rest.
To hoe up weeds in spring's my lot,
At dusk I water garden plot.
The magistrate knowing I've come
Orders me to learn to beat drum.
For service in my native land,
I need not carry things in hand.
Alone, I care not where to stay,
Be it near by or far away.
The land's in ruins and debris,
The distance means nothing to me.
Sick for five years, my mother died
Unburied, with none by her side.
She gave birth to me, is it wrong?
How to repay her all life long?
I have no home to say goodbye.
What can poor people do but sigh!

佳　人

绝代有佳人，
幽居在空谷。
自云良家子，
零落依草木[1]。
关中昔丧败，
兄弟遭杀戮。
官高何足论？
不得收骨肉[2]。
世情恶衰歇，
万事随转烛[3]。
夫婿轻薄儿，
新人美如玉。

① 依草木：在山中居住。

② 骨肉：一同受苦的兄弟。

③ 转烛：风中的烛火转动明灭，比喻世事无常。

《佳人》作于公元759年秋天，杜甫在安史之乱后辞官家居的时候。诗中的绝代佳人是个良家女子，兄弟都是高官，不幸在战乱中被害，自己又被喜新厌旧的丈夫遗弃，只得同侍婢幽居在空谷中。这位佳人的形象，在中国古典文学的人物画廊中，显得独特而且鲜明。她的命运非常悲惨，但是情操却又非常高洁。杜甫写她的命运时，用的是第一人称，语气直率酣畅，多用“赋”的手法；赞美她的人品时，用的却是第三人

A Fair Lady

The fairest lady in full bloom
Lives in a valley in deep gloom.
Born from a noble family,
She sinks into wild greenery.
Riots broke out on Central Plain,
Her brothers by ill luck were slain.
In vain were they officials high;
Their corpses still unburied lie.
The world cares not for those who fall;
With dying candle passes all.
"My husband's fickle, I'm afraid,
He took a new wife fair as jade.

称，笔调含蓄蕴藉，多用"比兴"手法。如用山中泉水之清，来比喻空谷佳人的品格；用补壁青萝的朴素，来显示她纯洁的心灵；用采来充饥的柏子，象征耐寒不凋的品质；用日暮常倚的翠竹，暗示挺拔劲节的操行。所以梁启超在《情圣杜甫》中说："这位佳人，身份是非常名贵的，境遇是非常可怜的，情绪是非常温厚的，性格是非常高亢的，这便是他（杜甫）本人的写照。"

合昏[1]尚知时，
鸳鸯不独宿。
但见新人笑，
那闻旧人哭？
在山泉水清，
出山泉水浊。
侍婢卖珠回，
牵萝[2]补茅屋。
摘花不插发，
采柏[3]动盈掬。
天寒翠袖薄，
日暮倚修竹。

① 合昏：夜合花，叶子早晨开傍晚合。

② 牵萝：拾树枝藤条。

③ 采柏：采摘柏树叶。

At dusk mimosa folds up leaves;
At night a lonely lovebird grieves.
He loves his new wife's smile so deep
That he hears not his old wife weep.
Clear water flowing from the fountain
Turns filthy when out of the mountain.
My maid's sold pearls that we may dine;
We mend our thatched cot with vine.
I pick for my hair no flowers sweet,
But handfuls of cypress seed to eat.
With cold shiver my thin sleeves green.
At dusk on long bamboo I'd lean."

梦李白

（二首其一）

死别已吞声，
生别常恻恻[①]。
江南瘴疠[②]地，
逐客无消息。
故人入我梦，
明我长相忆。
恐非平生魂，
路远不可测。
魂来枫林[③]青，
魂返关塞[④]黑。
君今在罗网[⑤]，
何以有羽翼？

① 恻恻：悲叹不已。

② 瘴疠：疾病，时疫。

③ 枫林：李白被放逐前往的地方多见枫树。

④ 关塞：杜甫流亡经过的秦州一带多见关塞。

⑤ 罗网：指法网。

公元 758 年李白流放夜郎，第二年春在白帝城遇赦，回到江陵。但是杜甫远在北方，不知此事，写了两首《梦李白》，这是第一首。这首记梦诗分别按梦前、梦中、梦后叙写。写梦之前先写别离，生离之前先说死别，以死别衬托生离，可见二人是生死之交。前四句写梦前，第五句不说梦见故人，却说故人入梦，而入梦又是有感于诗人的长久思念，

Dreaming of Li Bai

(I)

We stifle sobs on parting with the dead;
On parting with the living, tears are shed.
You're exiled to miasmic Southern shore.
How can you not send us news any more?
Last night you came into my dream anew;
This shows how long I am thinking of you.
I fear it was not your soul I did dream.
Could it go such long way o'er mount and stream?
When it came, green would maple forests loom;
When it went, dark mountains were left in gloom.
Now you are caught in net and bound with strings.
How can you free yourself with bound-up wings?

可见二人思念之深。梦中乍见而喜，转念而疑，继而生出忧惧，对梦中心理的刻画，十分细腻逼真。梦魂归去，诗人依然思念不已，唯恐水深蛟龙作浪，诗魂再陷龙潭，的确是至诚至真的文字。梁启超说得好：杜甫对李白“所感痛苦，和自己亲受一样，所以作出来的诗，句句都带血带泪”。

落月满屋梁，
犹疑照颜色[1]。
水深波浪阔，
无使皎龙得！

①颜色：指相貌。

The setting moon on rafters sheds its light;

I seem to see your beaming face as bright.

O monstrous billows where water is deep,

Don't wake up monsters and dragons asleep!

梦李白

（二首其二）

浮云[1]终日行，
游子[2]久不至。
三夜频梦君，
情亲见君意。
告归常局促，
苦道来不易。
江湖多风波，
舟楫恐失坠。
出门搔白首[3]，
若负平生志。
冠盖满京华，
斯人独憔悴。

① 浮云：比喻人飘游不定。

② 游子：指李白。

③ 搔白首：大概是李白的习惯动作。

前篇所写是诗人初次梦见李白的情景，此后又连续出现类似的梦境，于是诗人又有此后篇的咏叹。前篇写的是梦见李白后忐忑不安的心理，后篇写的是梦中所见李白的形象。前四句诉说对故人的情谊。君入我梦，我见君意，体现两人肝胆相照的深情厚谊。“告归”六句描绘梦中李白的形象：每当魂归时，总是局促不安，苦诉往来之不易和江上风波迭起，对舟楫为风浪所吞的担忧；走出门去时搔着满头白发，分明是对壮志

Dreaming of Li Bai

(II)

Wandering clouds can be seen all the day,
But you, a wanderer, are far away.
For three successive nights I dreamed of you,
This shows our friendship old and ever new.
Leaving in haste, you said you had to go,
It was not easy to come, as we know.
There might be perils on the lake or river,
A single man in a small boat should shiver.
On leaving me, you scratched your white hair,
Regretting your ideals vanish in air.
So many courtiers in the capital,
Why should you not find your place, not at all?

未酬宏图难展的怅然。对李白的多个侧面描写，使其犹在眼前。"江湖"两句，暗喻李白身处险境，抒发诗人与李白惺惺相惜之情。后六句是诗人梦醒后所发感慨：峨冠华盖权高位重者满京华都是，唯独这样一个风华绝代的人晚景凄凉，说什么天网恢恢。纵然一定会流芳百世，然而身后之事生前是看不到了。作者发出沉重的喟叹，寄托着对李白的崇高评价和深厚同情，也包含着诗人自己的无限心事。

孰云网恢恢?
将老身反累。
千秋万岁名，
寂寞身后事。

Who says there is justice under the sky?

How could you have been exiled so far? Why?

What is the use of fame which lasts so long

As people have sung the funeral song?

秦州杂诗

（二十首其七）

莽莽万重山，
孤城山谷间。
无风云出塞，
不夜月临关。
属国[①]归何晚？
楼兰[②]斩未还。
烟尘一长望，
衰飒正摧颜。

① 属国：指吐蕃的使臣。

② 楼兰：汉代西域的一个古代小国。

公元759年秋天，杜甫携眷西行，历尽千辛万苦来到秦州。寓居秦州期间，诗人写出了《秦州杂诗》，共20首，这是第七首。首联即壁立千仞，落孤城于层峦叠嶂之间，四周苍莽大山，更衬托其险要高峻之势。扼咽喉要道，守边塞重地，身处这样一个富有烽火气息的敏感边城，日常生活也多一丝警觉之感。颔联表面写景，实则意味边塞生活宁静的表象下暗流涌动，也表达了诗人对紧张的边防形势的深切关注。五、六句

On the Frontier

(VII)

Mountain on mountain towers far and near,

A lonely town garrisons the frontier.

Even without wind, cloud will sail the sky;

The moon on townwalls sheds twilight on high.

How could all the peace talks be held so late?

When could we conquer the barbarous state?

Gazing on the war flames far, far away,

My face would lose color at the decay.

用典，苏武出使匈奴，被扣留 19 年，归国后任典属国；傅介子以百人出使，取楼兰王首级。吐蕃趁唐内乱，夺取陇右、河西之地，才使秦州成为边防前线，大约这时有使臣出使吐蕃未还，而吐蕃侵袭的危机还未解除，所以诗人叹息国家衰弱，并对这种局势感到深深的忧虑。所以结尾诗人仿佛看到处处烟尘，战火弥漫，对国家衰落的担忧，使诗人不禁疾首蹙额。全诗蕴含着作者对国势日渐式微的悲凉之感。

天末怀李白

凉风起天末[1]，
君子意如何？
鸿雁几时到？
江湖秋水多。
文章憎命达，
魑魅[2]喜人过[3]。
应共冤魂语，
投诗赠汨罗。

① 天末：天边。

② 魑（chī）魅（mèi）：妖怪。

③ 过：失误。

这首诗当作于公元759年秋，当时诗人弃官远游客居秦州。李白流放夜郎途中遇赦，还至湖南，杜甫因赋诗怀念他。天末指秦州，因地处边塞，宛在天尽头。凉风骤起，诗人自己的窘迫困顿都按下不提，只一句略嫌局促的寒暄，只是这一句寒暄包含了多少沧桑事，所以不知从何说起，只得欲说还休。急切盼望的书信久久不至，江湖多险，故书信一日不至，诗人一日不能安心，更见诗人思之心切。五、六句说文才出众

Thinking of Li Bai from the End of the Earth

An autumn wind rises from the end of the sky.
What do you think of it in your mind and your eye?
When will the wild geese bring your happy news to me?
Could autumn fill the lake and the river with glee?
Good fortune never favors those who can well write;
Demons will ever do wrong to those who know what's right.
Would you confide to the poet wronged long ago
Your verse which might comfort his soul in weal and woe?

者总是命途多舛，小人奸佞最喜闻乐见的是好人之过。这两句诗道出了自古以来才智之士的共同命运，也是与李白同病相怜的心声。自然而然地，诗人想起了屈原，同样遭到谗言诬陷，后被放逐的爱国忠魂。他说李白应“投诗赠汨罗”，是对李白的高度肯定，这样一个人不被这个时代所欣赏，只能向命运相同的古时圣贤倾诉。此诗感情强烈，读来百转千回。

月夜忆舍弟[①]

① 舍弟：自己称呼弟弟的谦词。

戍鼓[②]断人行[③]，
边秋[④]一雁声。
露从今夜白，
月是故乡明。
有弟皆分散，
无家问死生。
寄书长不达，
况乃未休兵[⑤]。

② 戍鼓：边防驻军的更鼓。

③ 断人行：鼓声响起，宵禁开始。

④ 边秋：边塞的秋天。

⑤ 未休兵：战争还未停息。

《月夜忆舍弟》是公元759年所作。一般望月思亲多写所见，杜甫却写所闻戍鼓和雁鸣，使人觉得凄凉，可见杜甫匠心。说今夜露白，既是写景，又是点明时令；说故乡月明，看似写景，实是抒情，这样借景抒情，就化平板为神奇了。接着转入主题，说兄弟离散，生死难卜，既说“无家”，自然寄信也收不到；最后说“未休兵”，又和最初说的“断人行”前后呼应。全诗层次井然，结构严谨，写出兄弟情深，可见大家本色。

Thinking of My Brothers on a Moonlit Night

War drums break people's journey drear;
A swan honks on autumn frontier.
Dew turns into frost since tonight;
The moon viewed at home is more bright.
I've brothers scattered here and there;
For our life or death none would care.
Letters can't reach where I intend;
Alas! The war's not come to an end.

同谷七歌

（其七）

男儿生不成名身已老，
三年饥走荒山道。
长安卿相多少年，
富贵应须致身早。
山中儒生旧相识，
但话宿昔[1]伤怀抱。
呜呼七歌兮悄终曲，
仰视皇天白日速。

① 宿昔：昔日。

此诗写的是公元 759 年，杜甫应同谷县令之邀，从秦州出发历尽艰难到达同谷，而县令却嫌弃杜甫已弃官且穷困潦倒便避而不见。适逢大雪封山的隆冬季节，诗人衣食无着之下搭草屋栖身，眼见一家人饿病在床，无奈中长歌当哭，和着血泪写出了这组长诗，这是第七首，是组诗中最精彩的篇章。开头是叹穷嗟老的身世感慨，年近半百，名未成，身已老，转徙流离，老病穷愁，集中地抒发了诗人身世飘零之感。三、四句，

Seven Songs Written in Tonggu

(VII)

I am a man grown old without making a name.
Starved three long years, I trudge desolate mountain way.
In the capital young men have won wealth and fame,
It is all natural for them to have their day.
I meet a scholar in the hills, a friend of mine,
Talking about the past, we can give sigh for sigh.
Alas! I've sung all my seven songs, line by line;
Looking up, I see the sun sink in western sky.

追叙困居长安时，达官贵人中少年很多，这不能不使诗人发出愤激的讽刺之词："富贵应须致身早"，以看似劝人的口吻，表达对凭借父兄余荫谋取卿相的腐败政治的愤慨。诗人身处异常窘困的境地，感叹自己不幸的遭遇，忧国忧民的怀抱无法施展，因而和友人谈起的都是令人伤感的往事。诗人默默地收起笔望天，只见白日转移，向着西方天际快速飞驰，顿生迟暮之感，悲壮激烈之情在诗人心底涌起。

病　马

乘尔[1]亦已久，
天寒关塞深。
尘中老尽力[2]，
岁晚病伤心。
毛骨岂殊众[3]？
驯良[4]犹至今。
物微意不浅，
感动一沉吟[5]。

①尔：指马。

②老尽力：年老而力驰。

③殊众：不同于众人。

④驯良：和顺善良。

⑤沉吟：忧思。

《病马》大约也是公元759年杜甫因为马病而写的。诗中说：我骑你的日子很久了。不管天寒地冻，山高路远，你总是风尘仆仆，尽心尽力。到了年终，你却病倒了，教我如何不伤心呢！你的皮毛筋骨和别的马没有什么不同，不过你驯善地跟随我一直到了今天。你的身价并不高贵，但是对我如此情深义重，叫我如何能不感动？能不沉吟？这首诗充分表现了杜甫的人道主义精神，也可能是他借马比喻自己。

To My Sick Horse

You have been ridden long
Through cold, deep mountain pass.
In dust you toil along,
Sick at year's end, alas!
Is your coat not the same
As others? Meek till now,
You're dearer than your frame.
Can I not be moved? How?

野望

清秋望不极，
迢递[①]起层阴[②]。
远水兼[③]天净，
孤城隐雾深。
叶稀风更落，
山迥[④]日初沉。
独鹤归何晚[⑤]，
昏鸦已满林。

① 迢递：遥远貌。
② 层（céng）阴：重叠的阴云。
③ 兼：连着。
④ 迥（jiǒng）：远。
⑤ 归何晚：为何归来得晚。

如果说《病马》是借物咏人的诗，那么《野望》就是借景抒情的作品。开始总写野外的景色，一眼望去清旷无极，远远地却出现了层层阴云。尽管还是秋水共长天一色，但孤城已经笼罩在浓雾之中。西风一起，落叶飘零，太阳也沉到山坳里去了。孤独的白鹤归来时已经天晚，暮色昏昏欲睡，林中满是乌鸦聒噪之声。这阴云浓雾，西风落叶，夕阳昏鸦，都象征着当时的形势，而纯洁的归鹤则是诗人的化身。

Dim Prospect

Autumn presents a boundless view,
Far off dark masses loom in heap.
The sky blends into water blue,
The lonely town veiled in mist deep.
The wind strips trees of leaves again,
The sun beyond the mountains sinks.
So late comes back the snowy crane,
The wood's thronged with crows as dusk winks.

蜀　相

丞相[1]祠堂何处寻？
锦官城[2]外柏森森。
映阶碧草自春色，
隔叶黄鹂空好音。
三顾频烦天下计，
两朝开济[3]老臣心。
出师未捷[4]身先死，
长使英雄泪满襟。

① 丞相：诸葛亮。
② 锦官城：成都。
③ 开济：开创基业，周济艰危。
④ 捷：取胜。

公元 760 年春天，杜甫初来成都，看了诸葛丞相祠堂，写了这首《蜀相》。诗人先问“祠堂何处”，回答说“锦官（成都）城外”，翠柏森森，既是写景，又是写人，说诸葛亮和翠柏一样万古长青。接着又写映阶草绿，隔叶禽鸣，但加了个“自”字，就有绿草念人之意；又加了个“空”字。更是知音远去，好音谁听？不写人而人自见。接着知音出现：一个三顾茅庐，商量安定天下的大计；一个开国济世，显示辅佐先帝后主的忠心。可惜出师未捷身先死，后世英雄怎能不涕泪零零呢？杜甫以身许国，志在济世，自然也在后世英雄之内。这首七律写出了诗人对诸葛亮的景仰，可以说西蜀丞相就是他的楷模。

Temple of the Premier of Shu

Where is the famous premier's temple to be found?
Outside the Town of Brocade with cypresses around.
In vain before the steps spring grass grows green and long,
And amid the leaves golden orioles sing their song.
Thrice the king visited him for the State's gains and pains;
He served heart and soul the kingdom during two reigns.
But he died before he accomplished his career.
How could heroes not wet their sleeves with tear on tear!

戏题王宰画山水图歌

十日画一水，
五日画一石。
能事[①]不受相促迫，
王宰始肯留真迹。
壮哉昆仑方壶[②]图，
挂君高堂之素壁。
巴陵[③]洞庭日本东，
赤岸[④]水与银河通，
中有云气随飞龙。
舟人渔子入浦溆[⑤]，
山木尽亚洪涛风。

① 能事：十分擅长的事情。
② 方壶：神话中的仙山，此处指高山。
③ 巴陵：郡名。
④ 赤岸：泛指江湖的边岸。
⑤ 浦溆（xù）：岸边。

这是一首题画诗。公元 760 年，杜甫定居成都期间，认识四川著名山水画家王宰，应邀作此诗。十日一水，五日一石，区区数言，就刻画了王宰一丝不苟的创作态度，盛赞其大家风范，高超的技艺不愿受时间的催迫，留下真实的笔迹于人间。“巴陵”句中连举三个地名，一气呵成，力现江水起于洞庭，东流到海，源远流长，一泻千里。江岸水势浩瀚渺远，连接天际，

Wang Zai's Painting of Landscape

He spends five days to paint a stone
And ten to paint a stream alone.
He will not work when pressed,
So of his work we are deeply impressed.
How lofty mountains undulate from east to west!
The wall on which the picture hangs is blessed.
Water flows from Western mountains to Eastern Bay
Until it joins the Milky Way.
Waves rise like clouds with which the flying dragons play.
The frightened fishermen run far away,
All mountain forests bend to stormy sway.

水天一色，仿佛与银河相通，云气弥漫，似有蛟龙。狂风激流中，渔人正急急避舟岸边，大风吹得山上树木像波浪一样俯偃起落。其画面行云流水，波澜壮阔，构图宏伟，气韵生动。诗人高度评价王宰旷古未有的技法，并用极为精练的诗歌语言概括了我国山水画的表现特点："咫尺应须论万里"。面对如此美作，诗人惊叹不知怎样得来的并州快剪，将秀丽江水剪来一半。

尤工远势[1]古莫比，
咫尺应须论万里。
焉得并州快剪刀，
剪取吴淞半江水。

① 远势：指绘画中的构图背景。

He can paint landscape far and near:
On a foot of silk miles of hills appear.
Where could I get the sharpest scissor blade
To cut the scroll and make a river of white jade?

南　邻

锦里[1]先生乌角巾，
园收芋栗[2]未全贫。
惯看宾客[3]儿童喜，
得食阶除[4]鸟雀驯。
秋水才深四五尺，
野航恰受两三人。
白沙翠竹江村暮[5]，
相送柴门月色新。

① 锦里：锦江附近。

② 芋栗：长得像芋艿的橡栗。

③ 宾客：一作“门户”。

④ 阶除：台阶、门前的庭院。

⑤ 暮：一作“路”。

这是公元760年，作者的生活比较安定的时期，到南邻朱山人家造访，回家以后写下的诗作。前四句是诗人造访时的场景：主人锦里先生头戴隐士常戴的“乌角巾”；园子里种的芋头、栗子，都成熟该收了，生活虽然清贫，但是从其家中的氛围可以知道，主人是个安贫乐道之士，满足于眼下的田园之乐。见惯了宾客的孩子们也不怕生，笑脸相迎；连台阶上啄食的鸟雀见人来也不飞，一派人与自然和谐相处的安宁静谧氛围。转眼诗人就已逗留大半天了，夕阳西下，该回去了。门外小河水深不过四五尺，山村野渡的小船只能容纳两三人，主人送客上船。渐渐地，白沙、翠竹，连同村庄一同隐在这暮色中，而自家的柴门，在已经升起的明月照耀下显现出来。

My Southern Neighbor

My southern neighbor wears a black cornered hat,
There are chestnuts and taros in his garden flat.
His children smile to welcome guests they used to see,
Birds seeking food in his yard are not frightened to flee.
The stream is four or five feet deep before his door;
The tiny boat can take three passengers or four.
I leave his green bamboos and white sand when it's late,
He sees me off in moonlight at his garden gate.

狂　夫

万里桥西一草堂，
百花潭水即沧浪。
风含翠篠[1]娟娟净[2]，
雨裛[3]红蕖[4]冉冉香[5]。
厚禄故人书断绝，
恒饥[6]稚子色凄凉。
欲填沟壑唯疏放，
自笑狂夫老更狂。

① 篠（xiǎo）：细竹。

② 娟娟净：秀丽洁白之态。

③ 裛（yì）：滋润。一作“浥”。

④ 红蕖：粉红的荷花。

⑤ 冉冉香：阵阵的清香。

⑥ 恒饥：长时间挨饿。

此诗作于公元 760 年夏。前四句写草堂及浣花溪的美丽景色，令人陶然。斜风细雨之中，翠竹轻摇，竹叶上泛着水光；细雨润物，使荷花格外娇艳，暗香浮动。颔联有“微风燕子斜”“润物细无声”的意味，风之微雨之细都不言而喻。后四句是与此美景极不相称的残酷的生活现实。诗人初到成都时，靠故人接济，一旦故人断绝消息，他的家人就免不了挨饿了，颈联即写此事。即使身陷这样的窘境，诗人却像一个斗士般顽强，以近乎狂放的态度面对，诗人的这种人生态度，不但没有随同岁月流逝而衰退，反而越来越增强了，一句“自笑”，多少无处排遣的愁苦饱含其中。

Unbent Mind

West of the Bridge there stands my thatched hall,
Beside a pool where water plays with flowers.
The breeze caresses bamboos green and tall;
Pink lotus blooms moistened sweeten the bowers.
But unprovided for by my old friend,
My hungry children look haggard and drear.
Could I bow before I come to my end?
I laugh and hold my unbent mind as dear.

江　村[1]

① 江村：江畔的村庄。

清江[2]一曲抱[3]村流，
长夏江村事事幽。
自去自来[4]梁上燕，
相亲相近水中鸥。
老妻画纸为棋局，
稚子[5]敲针作钓钩。
多病所须惟药物[6]，
微躯此外更何求？

② 清江：清澈的江水。

③ 抱：环绕，围绕。

④ 自去自来：形容自由自在，无拘无束。

⑤ 稚子：幼子。

⑥ 一作“但有故人供禄米”。

《江村》是公元760年杜甫在成都西郊浣花溪畔修筑草堂后的作品。弯弯曲曲的锦江环抱着草堂流过，江畔小村在漫长的夏天显得非常幽静。村里的燕子在梁间飞来飞去，自由自在；江上的白鸥成对成双，相伴相随。老妻把纸画成棋盘，正好下棋消夏；儿子把针敲成鱼钩，清江可以垂钓。只是多病需要吃药，除此以外并无他求。诗中重复字多，如“江”“村”两见，“事事”叠现，还有“自去自来”“相亲相近”，但是错落有致，读来不嫌重复。全诗前后照应紧凑，结句转为凄婉，具有杜诗沉郁的特点。

The Riverside Village

The winding clear river around the village flows;
We pass the long summer by riverside with ease.
The swallow freely comes in and freely out goes;
The gulls on water snuggle each other as they please.
My wife draws lines on paper to make a chessboard;
My son knocks a needle into a fishing hook.
Ill, I need only medicine I can afford.
What else do I want for myself in my humble nook?

野　老[1]

① 野老：杜甫自称。

野老篱边[2]江岸回，
柴门不正逐江开[3]。
渔人网集澄潭[4]下，
贾客[5]船随返照来。
长路关心悲剑阁，
片云何意傍琴台？
王师未报收东郡，
城阙秋生画角哀。

② 篱边：竹篱的旁边。

③ 逐江开：描写浣花溪向东流去。

④ 澄潭：指百花潭。

⑤ 贾（gǔ）客：商人。

公元760年，经过长年的颠沛流离之后，杜甫在成都草堂定居下来，写下此诗。终于有了一个憩息之所的诗人，在此诗的前四句表达的是闲适隐逸的心情。然而江中的客船又扰乱了诗人平静的心，使他想起漫漫长路的那一端，是长安，还是洛阳？然而剑阁之内动荡离乱，音信全无，关山难越，与亲人梦魂阻隔，自己浮云般的漂泊之身，究竟为何滞留剑外呢？片云是诗人自喻，琴台相传为司马相如和卓文君当垆卖酒之地，此指代成都。此句流露出诗人寓居剑外，报国无门的愁苦。东郡，指洛阳。尾联两句叹洛阳二次失陷后，至今尚未光复，城楼传来的号角声也十分凄切悲凉，以声音做结尾，有余音绕梁的艺术效果。

An Old Man by the Riverside

A fence of bamboo winds along the riverside,
My wicket gate opens askew to greet the tide.
Fishermen set their nets in water clear and bright,
Merchant ships arrive with the departing sunlight.
The road is long to recover the whole lost land,
Why should the lonely cloud drift where no lutists stand?
The east is not yet in the hand of royal force.
I'm grieved to hear autumn bugle and neighing horse.

恨　别

洛城[1]一别四千里，
胡骑长驱五六年。
草木变衰行剑外[2]，
兵戈阻绝老江边。
思家步月清宵立，
忆弟看云白日眠。
闻道河阳近乘胜，
司徒[3]急为破幽燕。

①洛城：洛阳。

②剑外：指蜀地。

③司徒：指李光弼。

公元760年杜甫在成都写下此诗。首联作者通过空间和时间，以一己之身的遭遇，反映出国家的动荡局面和百姓的离乱之苦。诗人于剑外，眼见草木盛衰变易，枯荣交替，然而兵戈未息，不能重返故土，只得在这逝者如斯的江边渐渐老去。颈联突出题意，思家故夜不能寐，忆弟故怅然高卧，倦极而眠，委婉曲折地表现了怀念亲人的无限相思。尾联充满希望，诗人听到唐军连战连捷的喜讯，感到复国指日可待，自己也可还乡，所以充满希冀。

Separation

The capital is left four thousand li away,
For five or six years by Tartar steeds occupied.
Grasses and woods wither in the west day by day;
War flames prevent me from leaving the riverside.
Thinking of home, I pace with the moon all the night;
Longing for brothers while watching clouds brings sleep.
'Tis said the rebels are beaten with main and might;
We wish but victory be followed up far and deep.

后　游

寺忆曾[①]游处，
桥怜再渡时。
江山如有待[②]，
花柳自无私。
野润烟光[③]薄，
沙暄[④]日色迟。
客愁全为减，
舍此复何之？

① 曾（céng）：一作“新”，一作“重”。

② 待：有所期待。

③ 烟光：云霭雾气。

④ 暄（xuān）：暖。

杜甫于公元761年曾到新津，写下《游修觉寺》，第二次即写了这首《后游》。前四句回应往日之游而写后来之游，前两句采取倒装句式，有如老友重逢一般，对景物寄予深厚感情。美好江山似乎早已期待着老朋友的再次光临，花柳也很慷慨，诗人对山水花草富有感恩和喜爱之情，也从侧面说明了他在人世间的不得意。诗人是如此陶醉于自然，以至于从“烟光薄”到“日色迟”，流连于此，欣然忘返，又从侧面说明了景色之美。诗文以一句感慨结尾，得风景如此，漂泊在外的客愁全消，除了这还有什么地方可去呢？不只是赞风景绝佳，更是对山河破碎，民生凋敝，报国无门，忧愁难解的委婉表达。

The Temple Revisited

The memories of the temple still last.
Can I forget the bridge where I have passed?
The hill and stream still seem to wait for me;
To enjoy flowers and willows I'm free.
Morning sheds light and mist to feed the land;
The setting sunbeams won't leave beaming sand.
My homesickness vanishes in the air.
Where else can I cure my nostalgia? Where?

客　至

舍[①]南舍北皆春水，
但见群鸥日日来。
花径[②]不曾缘客扫，
蓬门[③]今始为君开。
盘飧市远[④]无兼味，
樽[⑤]酒家贫只旧醅[⑥]。
肯与邻翁相对饮，
隔篱呼取尽余杯。

① 舍：指家。

② 花径：长满花草的小路。

③ 蓬门：蓬草编扎的门户。用以指代简陋的房屋。

④ 市远：远离市集。

⑤ 樽：酒器。

⑥ 旧醅（pēi）：隔年的酒。

《客至》是公元761年杜甫在草堂待客的作品。先写环境，草堂南北都是浣花溪水，天天只见白鸥飞来，而白鸥是水边隐士的伴侣，这就点明了杜甫的隐居生活。花径未扫，蓬门始开，更说明了生活幽静。前半虚写客来之前，后半实写客来之后。草堂远离街市，买东西不方便，菜肴简单，酒也只有家酿的旧醅。但如果要"把酒话桑麻"，还可以请邻翁过来同饮。这首诗把门前景、家常话、身边事，编织成富有情趣的生活场景，是一首充满了人情味的叙事诗。

For a Guest

North and south of my cottage winds spring water green;
I see but flocks of gulls coming from day to day.
The footpath strewn with fallen blooms is not swept clean;
My wicket gate is opened but for you today.
Far from market, I can afford but simple dish;
Being not rich, I've only old wine for our cup.
To drink together with my neighbor if you wish,
I'll call him o'er the fence to finish the wine up.

绝句漫兴

（九首其一）

眼见客愁愁不醒[①]，
无赖[②]春色到江[③]亭。
即遣花开深造次[④]，
便觉莺语太丁宁。

① 愁不醒：难以排遣愁烦。

② 无赖：春意恼人。

③ 江：浣花溪。

④ 造次：仓促。

《绝句漫兴九首》写于杜甫寓居成都草堂的第二年（761）。“漫兴”就是兴之所至，随手写出，不求写尽，也不求写全的意思。这一首写诗人沉浸在飘零客居的愁思中，春色如懵懂无知的少女，莽莽撞撞地闯进了诗人的眼帘，就在诗人的眼前花团锦簇，莺啼婉转，更平添一层烦愁心绪。诗人善用反衬手法，深化情景对立，加强思想感情的表达。

Quatrains Written at Random

(I)

My eyes are unawakened to grief of spring,
Which beautifies still the riverside bowers.
Why should the talkative orioles sing
And my eyes be bewildered by blooming flowers?

绝句漫兴

（九首其三）

熟知茅斋[1]绝低小，

江上燕子故来频。

衔泥点污[2]琴书内，

更接飞虫打着人。

① 茅斋：茅屋。

② 点污：弄脏。

这一首景中含情，带有浓厚的生活气息，更透出一股闲适之意。给人自然、亲切之感。燕子往来穿梭，忙忙碌碌，相形之下诗人好整以暇，倒显出些许无奈与落寞。一说诗人通过对燕子频频扰人情景的描写，引出禽鸟也似欺人的感慨，表现诗人客居他乡的诸多烦恼和心绪不宁。

Quatrains Written at Random

(III)

Knowing my thatched hut small with roof low,
Swallows oft come across the stream and go.
They stain my lute and books with clods of clay
And knock at my head while catching its prey.

绝句漫兴

（九首其五）

肠断春江欲尽头，
杖藜徐步立芳洲[①]。
颠狂[②]柳絮随风舞，
轻薄桃花逐水流。

① 芳洲：花草丛生的水中洲陆。

② 颠狂：颠：一作“癫”。诗中形容放荡不羁的样子。

诗人要走到春江的尽头，为什么会“肠断”呢？可能是忧国忧家，也可能是惜春归去，所以放慢了脚步，拄着拐杖，站在芳草萋萋的洲头，看见柳絮如醉如狂，随风飞舞，桃花轻浮浪荡，顺水漂流。这既可以说是惜春归去，也可以说是借物讽人，写出了诗人的遐思漫想。

Quatrains Written at Random

(V)

The river's broken-hearted to see spring pass away;
Standing on fragrant islet, I ask spring to stay.
But willow down runs wild and dances with wanton breeze;
Peach blossoms frivolous go with the stream as they please.

绝句漫兴

（九首其七）

糁径杨花铺白毡，
点溪荷叶叠青钱。
笋根雉子[1]无人见，
沙上凫雏[2]傍母眠。

① 雉子：小鸡。

② 凫雏：小鸭子。

这首写初夏景色。作者漫步林溪之间，初夏的美妙自然令人流连，闲静之中，微含客居异地的萧寂之感。“糁径”指杨花散落的小径，好像铺上了一层白毡，“点”“叠”二字，把荷叶在水中的状态写得十分生动传神。这首诗语言朴实生动，意境清新隽永，景物相融，各得其妙。

Quatrains Written at Random

(VII)

The path paved with willow-down looks like carpet white;
The creek dotted with lotus leaves like coins blue.
Waterbirds young and old sleep on sand left and right;
The pheasants lie hidden at the foot of bamboo.

春夜喜雨

好雨[①]知时节，
当春乃发生[②]。
随风潜入夜，
润物细无声。
野径[③]云俱黑，
江船火独明。
晓看红湿处，
花重[④]锦官城[⑤]。

① 好雨：春雨。
② 发生：植物生长。
③ 野径：小路。
④ 花重：花沾了雨滴显得更饱满。
⑤ 锦官城：指成都。

《春夜喜雨》是杜甫的名作。开头一个“好”字，就把雨拟人化。雨“好”在哪里呢？第一好在适时，春天万物生长，正需要雨，雨就来了，多么“知时节”！第二“好”在“润物”，无声无息，造福天下，既不求名，也不讨好。这写的是所闻。下面再写所见：开门一看，天上阴云密布，地上水上一片漆黑，只有几点渔火闪烁，雨可能要下个通宵，这说明第三“好”在持久，又点明了是夜雨。最后写所想：明天一定满城花开，春意盎然，这还点明了“春”。诗写的是好雨，也表现了好人的品格。

Happy Rain on a Spring Night

Good rain knows its time right;
It will fall when comes spring.
With wind it steals in night;
Mute, it moistens each thing.
O'er wild lanes dark cloud spreads;
In boat a lantern looms.
Dawn sees saturated reds;
The town's heavy with blooms.

江亭

坦腹[①]江亭暖，
长吟野望时。
水流心不竞，
云在意俱迟。
寂寂[②]春将晚，
欣欣[③]物自私。
江东犹苦战，
回首一颦眉。

① 坦腹：仰卧，坦露胸腹。

② 寂寂：悄悄地。

③ 欣欣：繁盛的样子。

此诗作于公元761年，诗人居于草堂，生活暂时比较稳定。暮春时节，诗人仰卧江亭，吟诵着《野望》，此刻诗人的心境，是与世无争的，就像仅仅为了自然规律而流动飘卷的江水和白云一样。这两句诗不止是情景交融，更包含深刻的人生哲理。五、六句融景入情，诗人百般寂寥反怪万物自私，透露了万物兴盛而诗人独自忧伤的悲凉。国运衰微，江东战局艰苦，诗人每每回首，都愁眉不展。这首诗前四句写隐居生活的悠闲，后四句写对国家的担忧，表达诗人心怀天下，忧心国事的焦灼苦闷。

Riverside Pavilion

I lie supine by riverside,
And croon while gazing on fields wide.
With running water I won't vie;
My mind floats with the cloud on high.
Spring will soon be late in the gloom.
Why should flowers vie in full bloom?
The war is raging in the east.
Can I not frown with mind unreleased?

琴　台[1]

① 琴台：汉代司马相如弹琴遇见卓文君的地方。

茂陵[2]多病后，
尚爱卓文君[3]。
酒肆人间世，
琴台日暮云。
野花留宝靥[4]，
蔓草见罗裙。
归凤求凰意，
寥寥不复闻。

② 茂陵：司马相如生病后住在茂陵。

③ 卓文君：汉代的才女，与司马相如相识相爱。

④ 宝靥（yè）：笑脸。

此诗是杜甫晚年在成都凭吊司马相如奏《凤求凰》的琴台遗迹时所作。司马相如晚年退居茂陵，故这里以地名代之。首联是说尽管年华老去，多病缠身，司马相如对卓文君仍然怀着热烈的爱，引出颔联对他们年轻时代的追忆。二人不向世俗礼法屈服，开酒垆维持生计，诗人对他们非凡的勇气表示赞赏。诗人徘徊在琴台，对着暮霭碧云，暗自追怀。琴台旁美丽的野花，使作者联想到它仿佛是文君当年脸上的笑靥；嫩绿的蔓草，仿佛是文君昔日所着的碧罗裙，再现卓文君光彩照人的形象。尾联鲜明地点出主题，这种敢于挑战世俗，追求自由美好生活的精神，后世再无人继之了。

Wooing Lutist

The lutist ill but fine
Still loved the phenix proud.
In their shop they sold wine;
He played lute for the cloud.
Her dimple in full bloom,
And her skirt like grass green.
Where's the bride with her groom?
Nowhere can they be seen.

水槛[①]遣心

（二首其一）

① 水槛（jiàn）：水亭的栏杆。

去郭[②]轩楹[③]敞，
无村眺望赊[④]。
澄江平少岸，
幽树晚[⑤]多花。
细雨鱼儿出，
微风燕子斜。
城中十万户，
此地两三家。

② 去郭：远离城郭。

③ 轩楹：廊柱，此处指草堂的建筑物。

④ 赊（shē）：长，远。

⑤ 晚：指开花季节晚。

此诗大约作于公元761年。一番经营后，草堂园亩扩展了，树木多了。水亭旁，还添了专供垂钓、眺望的水槛。诗人这一时期的生活是安定闲适的。由于远离城郭，旁无村落，所以轩楹宽敞，视野开阔，良辰美景一览无余。上涨的江水碧澄清澈，几乎与岸齐平了，所以看不到江边堤面；树木郁郁葱葱，繁花竞相开放，在幽暗的黄昏中，散发出缕缕清香。细雨中鱼儿戏水，微风中燕子斜飞，这是历来为人传诵的名句。这一刻，诗人不只是热爱自然，更是融入于自然，故如此自然天成而不露雕琢之痕。这里只闲居着两三户人家，所以没有城中的喧嚣，也是诗人"风景这边独好"之感的由衷抒发。

Waterside Hermitage

(I)

Far from the town, my garden's wide;
No hut in view, I gaze afar.
Clear water levels riverside;
At dusk blooms look like star on star.
See fish emerge when rain is light,
And flying swallow clip the breeze.
Townhouse on townhouse out of sight,
I live in hermitage with ease.

茅屋为秋风所破歌

八月秋高风怒号，
卷我屋上三重茅[1]。
茅飞渡江洒江郊，
高者挂罥[2]长林梢，
下者飘转沉塘坳[3]。
南村群童欺我老无力，
忍能对面为盗贼。
公然抱茅入竹去，
唇焦口燥呼不得，
归来倚杖自叹息。
俄顷风定云墨色，
秋天漠漠向昏黑。

① 三重（chóng）茅：几层的茅草。

② 挂罥（juàn）：挂着。

③ 塘坳（ào）：池塘。

公元760年八月，风雨交加，风把杜甫草堂屋顶上的茅草吹走，雨从破屋顶上漏下来，于是诗人就写了这一首《茅屋为秋风所破歌》。全诗可以分为四节：第一节五句，句句押韵，音响宏大，读来如闻秋风咆哮。第二节五句，写村童穷苦，抱狂风吹落的茅草而去，诗人心急如焚，

My Cottage Unroofed by Autumn Gales

In the eighth moon the autumn gales furiously howl;
They roll up three layers of straw from my thatched bower.
The straw flies across the river and spreads in shower,
Some hanging knotted on the tops of trees that tower,
Some swirling down and sinking into water foul.
Urchins from southern village know I'm old and weak,
They rob me to my face without a blush on the cheek,
And holding armfuls of straw, into bamboos they sneak.
In vain I call them till my lips are parched and dry;
Again alone, I lean on my cane and sigh.
Shortly the gale subsides and clouds turn dark as ink;
The autumn skies are shrouded and in darkness sink.

但又无可奈何。第三节八句，写屋破又遭连夜雨的苦况。第四节五句，一、三句七字，二、五、六句九字，长句气势磅礴，由个人的艰苦联想到天下的寒士，迸发出奔放的激情和热烈的希望，显示了诗人博大的胸怀和崇高的理想。

布衾多年冷似铁，
娇儿恶卧踏里裂。
床头屋漏无干处，
雨脚如麻未断绝。
自经丧乱少睡眠，
长夜沾湿何由彻[①]！
安得广厦[②]千万间，
大庇[③]天下寒士俱欢颜，
风雨不动安如山！
呜呼！
何时眼前突兀[④]见此屋，
吾庐独破受冻死亦足！

① 何由彻：怎样支撑到早晨天亮。

② 广厦（shà）：宽敞高大的房屋。

③ 大庇：全部遮盖起来。

④ 突兀：形容房屋高高耸立的样子。

My cotton quilt is cold, for years it has been worn;
My restless children kick in sleep and it is torn.
The roof leaks o'er beds, leaving no corner dry;
Without cease the rain falls thick and fast from the sky.
After the troubled times troubled has been my sleep.
Wet through, how can I pass the night so long, so deep!
Could I get mansions covering ten thousand miles,
I'd house all scholars poor and make them beam with smiles.
In wind and rain these mansions would stand like mountains high.
Alas! Should these houses appear before my eye,
Frozen in my unroofed cot, content I'd die.

赠花卿

锦城[1]丝管[2]日纷纷[3]，
半入江[4]风半入云。
此曲只应天上有，
人间能得几回闻？

① 锦城：成都。
② 丝管：弦乐和管乐。
③ 纷纷：形容多。
④ 江：指成都的锦江。

花卿是花敬定，成都尹的部将，但是居功自傲，目无朝廷，僭用天子的音乐，所以杜甫这首诗对他进行了委婉的讽刺。开始说的“锦城”就是成都，“丝管”指的是管弦乐器，“日纷纷”是说日日演奏，音乐从花卿家里随风飞到锦江之上白云之间去了。前两句是实写，读来仿佛是对乐曲的赞美，其实有言外之意。后两句是虚写，说此曲只应天上有，而“天上”暗指天子。既然是天子用的音乐，人间的大臣怎么可以僭用呢？这不合乎礼制，在当时简直是大逆不道。所以这首诗和《丽人行》一样是寓讽于谀的。

To General Hua

With songs from day to day the Town of Silk is loud;
They waft with winds across the streams into the cloud.
Such music can be heard but in celestial spheres.
How many times has it been played for human ears?

不　见

不见李生[①]久，
佯狂[②]真可哀。
世人皆欲杀，
吾意独怜才[③]。
敏捷诗千首，
飘零酒一杯。
匡山读书处，
头白好归来。

① 李生：指李白。

② 佯（yáng）狂：故作颠狂的样子。

③ 怜才：爱惜有才之人。

这首诗写于客居成都初期，或许此时诗人辗转得知李白已在流放途中获释，故有感而作，此时自二人分别已16年。起首便言不见日久，并对李白只能以佯狂纵酒来表示对污浊世俗的不满感到深深的悲哀。当道朝廷的政客，都欲将其除之而后快，诗人对李白的遭遇满怀悲愤和同情，而诗人自己因疏救房琯被逐出朝廷，所以他非常理解李白的冤屈和苦衷，

Longing for Li Bai

I have not seen Li Bai for long,
Men of the world have done him wrong.
He can't but pretend to be mad.
How could a talent turn so sad!
At once he can write line on line;
What he asks for is cups of wine.
Come back to read, oh! In the height,
Let age snow on your head hair white!

有与其同病相怜之意。诗人赞李白才思敏捷，风华盖世，又叹其只能一生飘零，借酒消愁。所有的叹息和怀念，最后化为深切的呼唤。匡山位于四川境内，李白年少时曾读书于此，所以是叶落归根的好去处，而这时诗人客居成都，李白归来就能相见。诗以相见的渴望结尾，首尾呼应，抒发肝胆相照的深厚感情。次年，李白客死当涂，此诗遂成千古长叹。

江畔独步寻花

（七首其六）

黄四娘[1]家花满蹊[2]，
千朵万朵压枝低。
留连戏蝶时时舞，
自在娇莺恰恰啼。

① 黄四娘：杜甫的邻居。

② 蹊：小路。

公元760年杜甫新建草堂，春暖花开的时候，独自沿着江畔散步，写了七首绝句，这里选的是第六首。开头一句点明寻花的地点，是到黄四娘家去的路上；人名入诗，有点民歌的味道。“花满蹊”后，再说“千朵万朵”，更具体化；说“压枝低”，更形象化。蝶舞莺歌则写花的芬芳鲜艳。“留连”既是蝶恋花，也是人恋花和蝶；“自在”也既指莺，又可指人。“恰恰啼”有两说：一说是莺啼声，一说唐人口语“恰恰”是正好的意思。最后两句对仗工稳，因难见巧，和《漫兴》相同，可见杜甫诗艺。

Strolling Alone among Flowers by Riverside

(VI)

Along the Yellow Path flowers are overgrown,
Thousands of them in full blossom weigh branches down.
Butterflies linger, now and then they dance along;
Golden orioles warble with ease their timely song.

戏为[1]六绝句

（其二）

① 戏为：戏作。

王杨卢骆当时体，
轻薄为文哂[2]未休。
尔曹身与名俱灭，
不废江河万古流。

② 哂（shěn）：讥笑。

《戏为六绝句》是杜甫的六首文艺批评诗，这里选的是第二首。“王杨卢骆”是初唐诗人中的四杰：王勃、杨炯、卢照邻、骆宾王。“当时体”是当时的文体。“轻薄为文”一说是指批评者轻薄，一说是批评者认为四杰轻薄。“哂未休”是不断地嗤笑。“尔曹”指批评者。“江河”则比喻四杰，说他们的文名会流传万古。这首绝句别开生面，在小诗中发大议论，是前所未有的。读来情味盎然，如闻其声，如见其人，无论嬉笑怒骂，都能给人亲切之感，而又耐人寻味。

Six Playful Quatrains

(II)

Our four great poets write in a creative way;
You shallow critics may make your remarks unfair.
But your bodies and souls will fall into decay.
While their fame will last as the river flows fore'er.

闻官军收河南河北

剑外[1]忽传收蓟北，
初闻涕泪满衣裳。
却看[2]妻子愁何在，
漫卷诗书喜欲狂。
白日放歌须[3]纵酒，
青春[4]作伴好还乡。
即从巴峡[5]穿巫峡，
便下襄阳向洛阳。

① 剑外：剑门关外。

② 却看：回头看。

③ 须：应当。

④ 青春：春天青葱的景色。

⑤ 巴峡：推测是西陵峡。

公元 762 年冬天，唐军在洛阳附近打败了叛军，收复了黄河以南的地区，第二年春天，又收复了黄河以北的地区。杜甫这时还在剑门关外，听到消息，悲喜交集，就写了这首“生平第一快诗”。这种又惊又喜的情感洪流，只用“涕泪满衣裳”五个字来以形写神。接着又用“却看妻子”和“漫卷诗书”两个动作，引出“喜欲狂”的主题。下面再用“放歌”“纵酒”来

Recapture of the Regions North and South of the Yellow River

'Tis said the Northern Gate is recaptured of late;
When the news reach my ears, my gown is wet with tears.
Staring at my wife's face, of grief I find no trace;
Rolling up my verse books, my joy like madness looks.
Though I am white-haired, still I'd sing and drink my fill.
With verdure spring's aglow, 'tis time we homeward go.
We shall sail all the way through Three Gorges in a day.
Going down to Xiangyang, we'll come up to Luoyang.

进一步写“喜欲狂”的具体表现。“青春作伴”是指春天全家结伴还乡的狂想。最后一联包含四个地名：巴峡和巫峡、襄阳和洛阳，既有句内上下对，又有句外前后对，形成了工整的对仗。文势、音调迅急犹如闪电，表现了想象的飞驰。仇兆鳌在《杜少陵集评注》中引王嗣奭的话说：“此诗句句有喜跃意，一气流注，而曲折尽情，绝无妆点，愈朴愈真，他人决不能道。”

送路六侍御入朝

童稚[1]情亲四十年，
中间消息两茫然。
更为后会知何地？
忽漫[2]相逢是别筵[3]！
不分[4]桃花红似锦，
生憎柳絮白于棉。
剑南春色还无赖，
触忤[5]愁人到酒边。

① 童稚：小孩。

② 忽漫：忽然。

③ 别筵（yán）：饯别的筵席。

④ 不分：忿忿不满。

⑤ 触忤（wǔ）：冒犯。

这首诗作于公元763年春，这年正月，唐军收复幽燕，历经八年的安史之乱结束。但是动荡的时局并未因此平息，诗人早日还乡的愿望破灭。这首诗借聚合离散之情，写迟暮飘零的身世之感。儿时的旧友40年未见，又值动荡乱世，消息不通，然而孩提时的纯真友情并未归于淡忘。时间是这样的久，没能想到今生会有重新相见的一天，本是值得高

Seeing Secretary Lu off to Court

We were companions forty years ago.
What happened to us since then we don't know.
Now we meet again but only to part.
Where to renew our friendship grieves my heart.
I do not like peach blossoms red and bright,
Nor willow down like cotton soft and white.
Why should spring annoy me with scenes so fine?
What could the annoyed one do but drink wine?

兴的事，然而乍一相逢，即是别宴。转折之大，使相逢之喜尽化万千愁思。分别时都是孩提，再见面已然迟暮，又身处乱世，一切都无从说起，更知后会无期。眼前春色分明，诗人却恼春色无赖，触忤愁人。诗人将生死离别，离怀难遣表现得沉郁苍凉。

别房太尉[1]墓

① 房太尉：房琯，杜甫好友。官拜刑部尚书，病逝后追赠太尉。

他乡复行役[2]，
驻马别孤坟。
近泪无干土，
低空有断云。
对棋陪谢傅[3]，
把剑觅徐君。
唯见林花落，
莺啼送客闻。

② 复行役：一再地奔波。

③ 谢傅：指谢安。

房太尉即房琯，唐玄宗入蜀时拜相，为人正直，后为唐肃宗所贬。杜甫曾毅然上疏力谏，结果得罪肃宗，几遭刑戮。房琯罢相后，于公元763年拜特进、刑部尚书。在路遇疾，卒于阆州。两年后杜甫经过此地，写此悼亡之作。诗人四处奔波，风尘仆仆，来到孤坟前。从侧面反映了房琯晚年的坎坷和身后的凄凉。诗人在坟前洒下许多伤悼之泪，以至于身旁周围的土都湿润了。让诗人痛哭流涕的不仅是对逝者的哀伤，也是对自

At the Graveyard of Former Prime Minister Fang

Being on journey in a foreign land,
I stop my steed at your tomb and still stand.
Wet with tears, no soil in the yard is dry,
Even broken clouds would weep in the sky.
You might play chess with General Xie at ease;
I'd hang my sword in your yard green with trees.
I have only fallen flowers in view
To hear orioles sing their song of adieu.

身受尽苦楚而难以言表的悲痛。天低云断，空气里弥漫着愁惨凝滞之感。“对棋”句中，谢傅指东晋名将谢安，生前拜太傅，爱下围棋，借指房琯。“把剑”句用了一个典故，《说苑》载：吴季札聘晋过徐国，心知徐君爱其宝剑，等到他回来的时候，徐君已经去世，于是解剑挂在徐君坟前的树上而去。诗人以谢安的儒雅风流喻房琯，以延陵季子自比，表示对亡友的深情厚谊，虽死不忘。结尾营造一个幽静肃穆的氛围，显得余韵悠扬不尽。

登　楼

花近高楼伤客心，
万方多难此登临。
锦江春色来天地，
玉垒浮云变古今[①]。
北极朝廷终不改，
西山[②]寇盗莫相侵。
可怜后主还祠庙，
日暮聊为[③]梁甫吟[④]。

① 变古今：与古今一同变化。

② 西山：和吐蕃交界处的雪山，位于今四川省西部。

③ 聊为：不甘心但还是要这样做。

④ 梁甫吟：相传为诸葛亮所作古乐府曲名。

公元764年十月，杜甫客居成都已有五年。那时吐蕃攻陷长安，所以诗人写《登楼》时，说到“万方多难”和“西山寇盗”，甚至连登楼看花也感到伤心了。于是诗人凭楼远望，看见锦江春水从天边汹涌而来，玉垒山上的浮云忽聚忽散，正像从古到今的人世变幻一样。这两句一句写水，向空间开阔视野；一句写云，就时间驰骋遐思。诗人不免起了忧

On a Tower

It breaks my heart to see blooming trees near the tower.
The country torn apart, could I admire the flower?
Spring comes from sky on earth and greens River Brocade,
The world changes now as then like white cloud o'er Mount Jade.
O royal court, like polar star remain the same!
Invaders from the west, don't put our land in flame!
I'm sad to see the temple of the conquered king.
At dusk in praise of his minister I would sing.

国忧民之心，又从所见转到所想，希望大唐王朝如北极星一样永放光芒，希望西边的吐蕃不要兴兵入侵。但是皇帝昏庸，很像西蜀亡国之君刘后主，而自己却空怀济世之心，苦无献身之路，只能学诸葛亮诵《梁甫吟》了。全诗融自然景象、国家灾难、个人情思为一体，所以沈德潜说："气象雄伟，笼盖宇宙，此杜诗之最上者。"

绝　句

（二首其一）

迟日江山丽，
春风花草香。
泥融[1]飞燕子，
沙暖睡鸳鸯。

① 泥融：形容泥土湿润。

这一首五言绝句写于成都草堂。第一句“迟日”指春日，语出《诗经·七月》的“春日迟迟”，在这里可以理解为春日迟迟停留，舍不得离开秀丽的江山；春风一吹，花草生香，使江山更加秀丽。阳光普照，泥融土湿，燕子飞来衔泥筑巢；日照沙暖，鸳鸯成对成双，静卧洲上。全诗四句，通篇对仗，分写风和日暖、花草鸳鸯，是一幅色彩鲜明、生意勃发的初春景物图。

Quatrains

(I)

Over a beautiful scene the sun is lingering,
Alive with birds and sweet with breath of early spring.
To pick the thawing sod a pair of swallows fly;
Basking on the warm sand, two by two lovebirds lie.

绝　句

（二首其二）

江碧鸟[①]逾白，
山青花欲燃[②]。
今春看又过，
何日是归年？

① 鸟：指江鸥。

② 花欲燃：花红似火。

这一首上联写景，下联抒情。前两句说：漫江碧波荡漾，白鸟掠水飞翔，显得羽毛更白；满山青翠欲滴，鲜花盛开，红艳如火。上联十字，写了山水花鸟四景，又分别着上碧绿、青翠、火红、洁白四色，令人赏心悦目。后两句写的是主观感受：春末夏初，风景虽好，但是岁月荏苒，归家遥遥无期，就不免引起诗人漂泊的伤感了。这是一首见景生情之作。

Quatrains

(II)

Against blue water birds appear more white;

On green mountains red flowers seem to burn.

Alas! I see another spring in flight.

O when will come the day of my return?

绝　句

（四首其三）

两个黄鹂鸣翠柳，

一行白鹭上青天。

窗含西岭[①]千秋雪，

门泊[②]东吴万里船。

① 西岭：西岭雪山。

② 泊：停泊。

公元 764 年，杜甫随成都尹严武回到草堂，写了四首即景小诗，这是其中最著名的第三首。全诗是两联对仗句。上联写草堂周围新绿的柳枝上，成对的黄鹂在歌唱；在一碧如洗的晴空里，一行白鹭在自由地飞翔。两句中用了黄、翠、白、青四种鲜明的颜色，组成了一幅绚丽的图景。下联写凭窗远望西山雪岭，仿佛是画框中的一幅图画，岭上的积雪终年不化，已经积了千年万代。再开门一看，可以见到从东方来的停泊在江边的帆船，于是诗人不禁想坐船回到万里之外的故乡去了。这四句景语也是情语，表达了诗人复杂细致的内心思想活动。

Quatrains

(III)

Two golden orioles sing amid the willows green;

A flock of white egrets flies into the blue sky.

My window frames the snow-crowned western mountain scene;

My door oft says to eastward-going ships "Goodbye!"

宿　府

清秋幕府井梧[1]寒，
独宿江城蜡炬残。
永夜[2]角声悲自语，
中天[3]月色好谁看？
风尘荏苒音书绝，
关塞萧条行路难。
已忍伶俜[4]十年事，
强移栖息一枝安[5]。

① 井梧：井边的梧桐。

② 永夜：整夜。

③ 中天：半空中。

④ 伶俜（pīng）：流离失所。

⑤ 一枝安：暂时安顿下来。指作者前往幕府担任参谋一职。

此诗作于公元764年秋，当时作者在严武幕府中任节度参谋。前四句描写景物，景中含情；后四句抒发情感，情触景生，全诗情景交融。首句点“府”，次句点“宿”，长夜里悲笳哀角，自道乱世凄凉；晴空中月色皎洁，无奈好与谁看。这正是诗人独宿江城，晚景凄凉的写照。战乱经久不绝，故乡音书阔别，草木变衰关塞萧条，阻隔交通无路可归。诗人从动乱开始以来，10年间离乱飘零饱尝辛酸，如今却又被强拉到这幕府里。虽然宿府非作者自愿，但是严武是杜甫友人，曾接济过杜甫，所以诗人是为着酬知己才栖身帐下，到幕府不久，就受到幕僚们的嫉妒、诽谤和排挤，日子很不好过，加上辗转流离的苦闷，共同酿成此佳作。

Lonely Night in the Office

Well-side plane-trees shiver with cold in autumn clear;
By flickering candlelight I sleep sad and drear.
I can but speak alone to hear sad bugle song.
With whom can I watch the bright moon all the night long?
In time of war no letter comes from far away.
How can I go on the frontier my lonely way?
Having suffered for ten long, long years without glee,
I can't but seek a shelter on this lonely tree.

倦 夜

竹凉侵卧内，
野月满庭隅[①]。
重露成涓滴[②]，
稀星乍有无。
暗飞萤自照，
水宿[③]鸟相呼[④]。
万事干戈里，
空悲清夜徂[⑤]！

① 庭隅（yú）：庭院的角落。

② 涓（juān）滴：水滴。

③ 水宿：栖息在水边。

④ 相（xiāng）呼：相互叫唤。

⑤ 清夜徂（cú）：清静的夜晚流逝。

这首诗的构思布局精巧玲珑。全诗起承转合，井然有序。前六句全写自然景色，全然无倦意，但这细致入微的景物，恰恰说明诗人辗转反侧，彻夜不眠，或醒卧榻上，或披衣闲步，点明题中“倦”字意。最后两句直抒胸臆，也是对上文夜不能眠的解释：不能酣眠，皆为国事。其时，安史之乱平息未久，吐蕃又进犯中原，早已支离破碎满目疮痍的山河，再次陷入连绵战火。朝廷内奸佞当道，诗人也已年老，深感自己报国无门，只能空悲切。再回看其景，莫不饱含哀愁。

Depressed Night

The cool of bamboo invades my bed,
Wild moonlight in my yard outspread.
Drop by drop drips down heavy dew,
Flickering starlight fades from view.
A firefly lights its lonely way
While waterbirds wait for the day.
See war flames outspread far and near!
How could the night be still and clear?

禹　庙

禹庙空山里，
秋风落日斜[1]。
荒庭垂桔[2]柚，
古屋画龙蛇。
云气嘘青壁[3]，
江[4]声走白沙。
早知乘四载，
疏凿控三巴[5]。

① 落日斜：落日西斜。

② 桔：一作“橘”。

③ 青壁：空旷的墙壁。

④ 江：大禹庙所在山崖下的长江。

⑤ 三巴：指蜀地的巴东郡、巴郡、巴西郡一带。传说是大禹治水后浮现的陆地。

公元765年，杜甫出蜀东下，途经忠州（今四川忠县），特地前去观览大禹古庙。荒凉空山之中，瑟瑟秋风正起，晚霞余晖，涂染这空旷寂静的山谷，更显古庙深幽阒寂，肃然独峙。庭中桔柚硕果垂枝，壁上古画龙蛇飞舞。这里暗含典故，据《尚书·禹贡》载，禹治洪水后，人民得以安居生产，远居东南的“岛夷”之民也“厥包桔柚”，把丰收的桔柚包裹好进贡给禹。又有传说，禹“驱龙蛇而放菹”，使龙蛇也有所

The Temple of Emperor Yu

In mountains void the temple shines;
In autumn breeze the sun declines.
In dreary yard fruits hang and fall,
Dragons and snakes dance on the wall.
Through mossy cliffs float mist and cloud,
The foaming river's rolling loud.
Yu went high and low, far and nigh,
To conquer the flood under the sky.

归宿，不再兴风作浪。青山千仞，云吞雾吐；白浪淘沙，东奔三峡。禹乘四种载具治水，凿通三峡的故事人所共知，而眼前的景象，引人追忆千年以前的上古洪荒，大禹不畏艰险凿石开山时的磅礴气势。诗人在山河破碎，风雨飘摇的时候歌颂大禹敢于征服自然的精神，意在希望君王能像大禹那样力挽狂澜，救民于水火，重振山河。诗人一片苦心，可昭日月。

旅夜书怀

细草微风岸，
危[①]樯[②]独夜舟。
星垂[③]平野阔，
月涌大江流。
名岂文章著？
官应老病休[④]。
飘飘何所似？
天地一沙鸥。

① 危：高。

② 樯：桅杆。

③ 垂：低垂。

④ 官应老病休：一说反语，应为“老病应休官”。

公元765年，杜甫因为严武去世，失去依靠，携家离开成都草堂，坐船东下，在渝州一带写了这首五言律诗。诗的前半写“旅夜”。第一句写近景：微风吹拂着江岸上的细草，竖着高高桅杆的小船孤独地停泊在月光之下；自己也像细草一样渺小，像江中小船一样孤独。第三、四句写远景：明星低垂，平野广阔，月随波涌，大江东流。这两句写景雄

Mooring at Night

Riverside grass caressed by wind so light,
A lonely mast seems to pierce lonely night.
The boundless plain fringed with stars hanging low,
The moon surges with the river on the flow.
Will fame ever come to a man of letters
Old, ill, retired, no official life betters?
What do I look like, drifting on so free?
A wild gull seeking shelter on the sea.

浑阔大，反衬出诗人的孤苦伶仃和颠沛无告的心态，这是以乐景写哀情的手法。诗的后半“抒怀”。第五、六句说，有点名声，哪里是因为我的文章好？做官，倒应该年老多病就退休了。最后两句说，飘然一身像个什么呢？不过像广阔天地间的一只沙鸥罢了。这样借景抒情，表现了诗人漂泊无依的心理状态，令人感慨系之。

八 阵 图[①]

① 八阵图：用石头垒成天、地、风、云、龙、虎、马、蛇八阵，用于操练或作战。诸葛亮曾布过此阵。

功盖三分国，
名成八阵图。
江流石不转，
遗恨失吞吴。

《金圣叹选批杜诗》中说：“八阵图，垒石作八行，在鱼腹浦平沙上：一天，二地，三风，四云，五飞龙，六翔鸟，七虎翼，八蛇蟠，为八阵。”八阵图的遗址在夔州西南永安宫前的平沙上，聚细石成堆，高五尺，六十围，纵横棋布，排列为六十四堆。公元766年，杜甫初到夔州，看见了八阵图，就写了这首诗。第一句说，诸葛亮的大功是使蜀和吴、魏三分天下。第二句说，他的军事贡献体现在对抗吴魏的八阵图上。第三

The Stone Fortress

With his exploits history is crowned;
For his Stone Fortress he's renowned.
The river flows but stones still stand,
Though he'd not taken back lost land.

句说，即使长江大水淹没平沙，水退之后，八阵图的石堆依然如故，600年来岿然不动。第四句说，诸葛亮的八阵图本是用来联吴抗魏的，但是刘备却要“吞吴”，于是金圣叹说：“不谓关羽奋一朝之勇，‘失’之于先；先主（刘备）又逞一击之忿，‘失’之于后。不能亲吴则亦岂能拒魏哉！”所以统一大业中途夭折，成了千古遗恨。这首绝句融议论入诗，把怀古与述怀合为一体，使人有此恨绵绵，余意不尽之感。

秋　兴

（八首其一）

玉露凋伤枫树林，
巫山巫峡气萧森。
江间波浪兼天涌，
塞上[①]风云接地阴[②]。
丛菊两开他日泪，
孤舟一系故园[③]心。
寒衣处处催刀尺[④]，
白帝城高急暮砧[⑤]。

① 塞上：指巫山。
② 接地阴：风云像要压到地面上。
③ 故园：指长安。
④ 催刀尺：赶裁新衣。
⑤ 急暮砧(zhēn)：黄昏时捣衣声急促。

《秋兴八首》是公元766年杜甫旅居夔州时的作品。这一首前半写所见（秋）：白露使枫叶凋残了，巫山和巫峡都是阴森森的；长江的波浪从下而上涌向天空，巫山的风云从上而下压得地面也阴暗了。这四句通过对秋色秋声的形象描绘，烘托出阴沉萧森、动荡不安的环境气氛，引起了诗人忧国之情和抑郁之感。后半接着就写所感（兴）：堆堆黄菊已经开过两次，菊上的白露就像他日的眼泪；一条孤零零的小船系住了诗人思念故园之心。家家户户都用刀尺裁剪冬衣，日暮天黑，又从白帝城传来了捣衣之声，更使人兴起了故国之思。这首诗由眼前所见萧条的秋色、所闻凄清的秋声，而引起对个人身世与国家命运的感叹，悲壮苍凉，意境深远。

Reflections in Autumn

(I)

The pearllike dewdrops wither maples in red dye;
The Gorge and Cliffs of Witch exhale dense fog around.
Waves of upsurging river seem to storm the sky;
Dark clouds o'er mountains touch their shadows on the ground.
Twice full-blown, asters blown off draw tears from the eye;
Once tied up, lonely boat ties up my heart home-bound.
Thinking of winter robes being made far and nigh,
I hear at dusk but nearby washing blocks fast pound.

秋　兴

（八首其二）

夔府孤城落日斜，
每依北斗望京华[1]。
听猿实下三声泪，
奉使虚随八月槎[2]。
画省[3]香炉违伏枕，
山楼[4]粉堞[5]隐悲笳。
请看石上藤萝月，
已映洲前芦荻花。

① 京华：指长安。

② 槎（chá）：木筏。

③ 画省：指尚书省。

④ 山楼：白帝城楼。

⑤ 粉堞（dié）：用白粉刷的矮墙。

第二首写夔府秋夜北望京华。首联承接上首尾联，由薄暮入笔。夔州地处群山之间，又值落日斜照，这深秋黄昏的景色对于一个命运坎坷、沦落天涯的人来说，更会引起落寞思乡之情。于是每当金乌西坠、玉兔东升时，诗人就依北斗星的方向眺望日夜思念的长安。望而不见，焉能不悲？旧时曾知在巫峡听猿声使人哀伤落泪，现在身在夔州，听到猿声实在伤感不禁泪下。肃宗上元二年（761），严武以兵部侍郎出任为成都尹兼御史大夫。杜甫希望能有机会随严武一同入朝，回到长安，实现其

Reflections in Autumn

(II)

The sun on the decline sinks behind the lonely town,
Seeing the Polar Star, I think of the Royal Crown.
Hearing the monkeys wail, can my tears not fall down?
How could I cross the Milky Way to find my own?
I cannot feel the royal incense from my bed,
Behind townwalls I hear sad bugle songs outspread.
Oh, look! With ivy on the rock the moon is fed,
It shines on weeds and reeds now at the riverhead.

政治理想。但不幸严武突然去世，八月份乘船回长安供职的心愿化为泡影。回长安如同乘浮槎至天河一般，茫茫不可达。“画省香炉”指在尚书省轮流值班，是诗人心中所向。卧病在床，不能回到朝中供职，只挂了个空衔，诗人正为没有机会报效国家遗憾愁闷，远处白帝城的城垛上隐隐约约传来凄咽的号角声，情极凄切缠绵，无限悲凉。尾联写月亮从照着藤萝移到照映着洲前芦荻花上，描写了夔州萧条的秋色，也暗示时间的推移，含有无限情思。

秋　兴

（八首其三）

千家山郭静朝晖，
日日江楼坐翠微[①]。
信宿[②]渔人还泛泛，
清秋燕子故飞飞。
匡衡抗疏[③]功名薄，
刘向[④]传经心事违。
同学少年多不贱，
五陵衣马自轻肥[⑤]。

① 翠微：青山。

② 信宿：再宿，连住两夜。

③ 抗疏：指臣子对皇帝的命令有所抵制，上疏劝谏。

④ 刘向：字子政，汉朝经学家。

⑤ 轻肥：轻裘肥马。

第三首是第二首的延伸，紧接上文的暮色写晨曦中的夔州。诗人日日独坐江楼，秋色清明，江水宁静，带给诗人的却是烦扰不安。每当山城的千家百户还沉浸在朝晖中，自己却孤身一人坐在江边山楼上，看着留宿江中的渔船，总是在上下翻飞的燕子，流露出诗人烦恼的心情。颈联用典，汉元帝初时，日蚀地震，匡衡上疏，帝悦其言，迁为光禄大夫，太子少傅，建议亦常被采纳；东汉刘向，在朝历经三世，都得重用，对儒学传播起了很大的作用。诗人将自己与匡、刘对比，叹息自己一生事与愿违。尾联用同学多不贱反衬自己的落魄不得志。

Reflections in Autumn

(III)

Thousands of mountain cottages bathed in the twilight,
Each day by riverside I gaze on verdant scene.
Fishermen come to cast their net after the night,
And swallows flap their wings and flit in autumn green.
Disposed after my proposal, I don't care for fame;
Studying classics, I am not yet a good hand.
Most of my young companions have made a fine name;
Splendidly clad, they ride splendid steeds on the land.

秋　兴

（八首其四）

闻道长安似弈棋，
百年[①]世事不胜悲。
王侯第宅[②]皆新主，
文武衣冠异昔时[③]。
直北关山金鼓振[④]，
征西[⑤]车马羽书驰[⑥]。
鱼龙寂寞秋江冷，
故国平居有所思。

① 百年：人的一生。

② 第宅：府宅。

③ 异昔时：不同往日。

④ 金鼓振：发生战事。

⑤ 征西：与吐蕃之间的战事。

⑥ 驰：形容紧急。

这一首是感叹长安时局多变以及边境纷扰。广德年间，吐蕃、回纥不断入侵，京师震撼，并曾一度占领长安，代宗仓促幸陕。是时诏征天下之兵，因宦官程元振专权，莫有至者。组诗由此首开始，主题转向回忆长安。首联说长安政局像棋局一样变化无常，自己一生见证了风雨飘摇，联想自己的浮生身世，心中满是悲苦。时局动荡，官员更替，满朝

Reflections in Autumn

(IV)

The change in capital's like a game on chessboard.
How sad to know what's happened in a hundred years!
New tenants occupy the mansions of old lord;
Officials and officers are not old compeers.
On Northern frontiers clash of gong vies with drumbeat;
Dispatch-riders hurry along their western way.
In autumn river quiet fish and dragon meet.
How can I not think of the splendid bygone day!

文武都是新人，本就备受冷遇的自己更加无所适从。西北多事，报军情的文件来往驰送，时局危急。尾联写在这国家残破、秋江清冷、飘零困苦、晚景凄凉的情况下，昔日在长安的生活常常呈现在怀想之中。表达诗人对人物皆非，盛世难再的叹惜与无奈。

秋　兴

（八首其五）

蓬莱宫阙[①]对南山，
承露金茎霄汉间。
西望瑶池降王母，
东来紫气满函关[②]。
云移[③]雉尾开宫扇，
日绕龙鳞[④]识圣颜。
一卧沧江[⑤]惊岁晚，
几回青琐点朝班[⑥]！

① 蓬莱宫阙：指大明宫。

② 函关：函谷关。

③ 云移：把宫扇比作云，像云一样散开。

④ 日绕龙鳞：形容皇帝衮袍上的龙纹光彩照人的样子。

⑤ 卧沧江：在夔州养病。

⑥ 点朝班：指上朝时，点名传呼百官依次上朝面圣。

这首承接上文，描绘长安宫殿的巍峨壮丽，早朝场面的庄严肃穆，以及自己曾得“识圣颜”至今引为欣慰的回忆。值此沧江病卧，岁晚秋深，更加触动他的忧国之情。蓬莱宫阙，即大明宫，唐高宗时改为蓬莱宫。南山，即终南山，山上有含元殿、宣政殿、紫宸殿，与蓬莱宫相对。承露金茎即通天台。汉武帝在建章宫西边作承露盘，上有仙人掌，用于承接露水，和玉屑饮用，以求成仙。诗歌的首联描写长安宫殿的景色，既是景物的描

Reflections in Autumn

(V)

The fairy palaces face Southern Mountains high,
The gold plate welcomes the dew fallen from the sky.
The Western Queen comes to the Pool of Emerald;
The Eastern Pass sees purple mist veil Master Old.
The royal fans of phoenix tails usher like cloud
The robe of dragon scales with sunbeams overflowed.
I lie by riverside till the end of the year.
How long from the court audience did I disappear!

写，也是暗指唐玄宗好道教求神仙的荒唐。颔联则用西王母和老子出函谷关的典故进一步指出，唐玄宗因为崇奉道教、追求长生而导致国家混乱。颈联联系到自身，感慨自己没有能尽力劝谏君王，于是想到自己在朝为官时的景象，“忠君爱国”的思想又充斥着诗人的胸怀。尾联写诗人虽然豪情万丈，但身居夔州，远离朝廷，加上年老多病，这一辈子是没有希望再去朝廷替皇上分忧解难了，寄托了人已老去，壮志难酬的感叹和哀伤。

秋　兴

（八首其六）

瞿塘峡[1]口曲江[2]头，
万里风烟接素秋。
花萼夹城通御气，
芙蓉小苑入边愁[3]。
珠帘绣柱围黄鹄[4]，
锦缆牙樯[5]起白鸥。
回首可怜歌舞地，
秦中自古帝王州。

① 瞿塘峡：峡名，三峡之一。

② 曲江：地名，在长安的南边。

③ 入边愁：传来边地战乱的消息。

④ 黄鹄：鸟名，即天鹅。

⑤ 锦缆牙樯：带有华丽装饰的游船。

本篇慨叹安史之乱以来，长安城满目疮痍。诗人在万里之外的瞿塘峡口，回想往日玄宗游幸曲江的盛况，对“自古帝王州”昔盛今衰的变化，不胜感慨。瞿塘为三峡门户，最险。曲江池，唐开元中疏凿，号为胜景。首联写如今万里唐家江山，全都淹没在这绵延万里的战火风烟之中。瞿塘峡与曲江口也接在这瑟瑟秋天的烽烟之中。花萼夹城，玄宗即位后，于兴庆宫西置楼，名曰花萼相辉之楼。后又筑夹城，天子游玩芙蓉园，必得

Reflections in Autumn

(VI)

Between the narrow Gorge and Winding River head
For miles and miles mild autumn breeze and mist out spread.
The royal way goes between walls with flowers in bloom.
To Lotus Hall where comes news of frontier in gloom.
The golden crane amid pillars and pearly screen,
Silver-white gulls around ivory masts or between.
What pity to see these places of dance and song
Where none of emperors or kings can reign for long!

从花萼楼夹城通过，故曰"通御气"，及后安禄山攻陷长安，作者羁身此地，望得山河破碎，故起边愁。颈联两句写当日皇帝游览之盛况，暗写今日江山之凋敝，昔盛今衰对比之中，可见作者的情怀。尾联歌舞地指曲江，秦中指长安，周秦汉隋都在此建都，秦州本帝王之州，今竟然以歌舞之故失去江山，实为可怜。金圣叹说这句有奉劝安禄山等国贼之意，秦州自古乃帝王之州，岂是逆贼可久居之地，暗示对来者的期待。

秋　兴

（八首其七）

昆明池[1]水汉时功，
武帝[2]旌旗在眼中。
织女机丝虚夜月，
石鲸鳞甲动秋风。
波漂菰[3]米沉云黑，
露冷莲房坠粉红[4]。
关塞极天惟[5]鸟道，
江湖满地一渔翁[5]。

① 昆明池：遗址在今陕西省西安市西南斗门镇一带，汉武帝所建。

② 武帝：此处代指唐玄宗。

③ 菰（gū）：即茭白，生在浅水中的草本植物。

④ 坠粉红：形容莲蓬成熟后，花瓣坠落的样子。

⑤ 惟：一作“唯”。

⑥ 渔翁：杜甫自比。

本篇写长安城昆明池盛衰变化，自伤漂泊江湖。这首诗以精丽的语言、生动的形象，在回忆昔日长安盛况的同时，抒发了自己旅居夔州欲归不得的感慨。诗的开头两句，借汉指唐，用想象中的威武场面颂扬了盛唐的强大。接下来四句的描写，似乎是写景，其实是对今日的荒凉冷落的一种喟叹。因此结尾两句，不仅实写关塞险阻，而且含有表达政治上的艰难处境的意思。所以诗人说自己是漂泊江湖的一个渔翁，暗喻自己漂泊无归宿，这样来表现自己处境的凄凉，形象而又真切。这首诗既抒发了忧国的情思，也感叹了自己可悲的命运。

Reflections in Autumn

(VII)

The Kunming Lake reminds us of the glorious day.
But Emperor Wu's flags cannot forever sway.
The Weaving Maiden seems to weave night with moonbeams,
The stone whale would exhale autumn breeze from its scale.
Wild seeds float on the waves as clouds darken the sky;
Cold dew chills lotus blooms falling in rosy dye.
We can go by a narrow path to the frontier,
I'd be a fisher to whom stream and lake are dear.

秋　兴

（八首其八）

昆吾御宿自逶迤[①]，
紫阁峰阴入渼陂[②]。
香稻啄余鹦鹉粒，
碧梧栖老凤凰枝。
佳人拾翠[③]春相问[④]，
仙侣[⑤]同舟晚更移[⑥]。
彩笔昔曾干气象，
白头吟望苦低垂。

① 逶迤（wēi yí）：道路、河道等弯且长的样子。

② 渼陂（bēi）：湖泊名，位于今陕西省西安市鄠邑区涝河西畔。

③ 拾翠：拾起翠鸟羽毛。

④ 相问：互赠礼物。

⑤ 仙侣：好伴侣。

⑥ 晚更移：指天色已晚，要乘船前往别处尽兴游玩。

此诗回想昔日在长安畅游渼陂之情境，慨叹青春献赋之豪情不再。诗人回忆在长安时与友人同游渼陂，首联即忆行踪，从长安出发，经过昆吾、御宿两地，再沿紫阁峰北面的山路而达于渼陂。颔联以写渼陂物产之丰，以及景色之美。颈联记渼陂泛舟的盛事。结尾以当年才华横溢反衬今日才思枯竭，言外有无穷感慨。诗人在盛衰今昔的巨大背景和心理反差中，不仅对唐王朝盛衰引起哲理性思考，更感到人生变幻无常，追忆昔日的风光之余，只能“白头吟望苦低垂”而已，通过强烈对比，表达对昔日如梦繁华的深沉缅怀，并抒发对盛衰交替，盛世难再的愁苦无奈。

Reflections in Autumn

(VIII)

To Royal Residence it is a winding way,
The purple peaks cast on the lake their shadows gray.
Parrots can't peck up all the grains left on the plain;
Phoenix when old on the plane tree will still remain.
Fair maidens gather vernal flowers with sweet smiles;
Boating with immortals would shorten evening miles.
While young, I had a magic brush to paint the scene.
What can I do now my age is no longer green?

咏怀古迹

（五首其三）

群山万壑赴荆门，
生长明妃[①]尚有村。
一去紫台[②]连朔漠，
独留青冢[③]向黄昏。
画图省识[④]春风面[⑤]，
环佩空归月夜魂[⑥]。
千载琵琶作胡语，
分明怨恨曲中论。

① 明妃：指王昭君。

② 紫台：汉宫，宫廷。

③ 青冢：指王昭君的坟墓。

④ 省（xǐng）识：指粗略识别。

⑤ 春风面：形容王昭君的美貌。

⑥ 月夜魂：一作“夜月魂”。

《咏怀古迹》也是公元766年杜甫旅居夔州时的作品，共五首，这里选的是第三首。诗人从三峡西头的白帝城向东远望，只见群山起伏如波涛滚滚奔向荆门的昭君村。但是村在人亡，昭君早已离开汉宫去了无边无际的北方沙漠，现在只剩下孤零零的青冢，对着笼罩四野的黄昏。假如当年画师画出了她的青春美貌，就不至于月夜思念亲人，孤魂在环

Thoughts on a Historic Site

(III)

All mountains rise and fall till they reach Thatched Gate,
'Tis the home village where was born the Lady Bright.
She left the palace for the desert desolate,
Her lonely tomb still green is left to face twilight.
No picture could portray her face as fair as spring's,
In vain her roving soul returned beneath the moon.
The pipa's sighed for ages on Tartarian strings,
We can discern her bitter grief in its sad tune.

佩声中不远千里回到故园了。几百年来琵琶奏出的哀曲，都是昭君在诉说她的怨情。当时杜甫也远离故乡，欲归不得，和昭君的境遇有相似之处，所以就借他人的酒杯，浇自己的块垒了。昭君身行万里，冢留千秋，心与祖国同在，名随诗乐长存，她的悲剧在读者心中留下了难以磨灭的印象。

阁　夜

岁暮阴阳催短景，
天涯霜雪霁[1]寒宵。
五更鼓角声悲壮，
三峡星河影动摇。
野哭[2]千家闻战伐，
夷歌数处起渔樵。
卧龙跃马终黄土，
人事音书[3]漫[4]寂寥。

① 霁 (jì)：雨雪停。

② 野哭：形容哭声遍野。

③ 音书：亲友间的音讯，书信等。

④ 漫：徒然，白白地。

公元 766 年，杜甫旅居夔州西阁，写了这首《阁夜》。开始两句点明时间，“岁暮”指冬天，“阴阳”指日月，“短景”指冬天日短，“催”字使人觉得岁月催人老。第二句的“天涯”指夔州，霜雪方停，寒光明朗如昼，对此夜景，诗人不禁感慨万千。第三、四句写五更时分，鼓角之声分外悲壮；天上银河映照在峡江中，摇曳不定，衬托着诗人深沉的情怀。第五、六句加重写所闻，一听说征伐之事，立刻引起千

Night in My Bower

By the year's end the day grows short to lengthen night,
I'm far from home where snow and frost turn the earth white.
I hear drear horns and drums announce the dawning day,
Mirrored in the Three Gorges, shivers the Milky Way.
Thousands of rural homes weep to know war prolong,
Where can woodsmen and fishermen sing their folk song?
Premier and Emperor were buried underground.
What matters if we live lonely or safe and sound?

家恸哭，这是时代的哭声；江边林中，又传来了渔歌和樵唱，这是地方的歌声。诗人极目远望，看到西郊的武侯祠和东南的白帝庙，想起诸葛亮和“跃马而称帝”的公孙述，都是一世之雄，而今安在？自己没有得到亲友音书，感到寂寥，相形之下，算得了什么呢！这首诗从当前现实写到千年陈迹，气象雄阔，仿佛把宇宙纳入毫端，有上天下地、俯仰古今之概。

孤　雁

孤雁不饮啄[1]，
飞鸣声念群。
谁怜一片影，
相失万重云[2]？
望尽[3]似犹见，
哀多如更闻。
野鸦无意绪，
鸣噪[4]自纷纷。

① 饮啄：鸟喝水和觅食。
② 万重云：形容云海茫茫。
③ 望尽：望到天尽头。
④ 鸣噪：野鸦啼叫。

《孤雁》作于公元765年杜甫旅居夔州期间。诗人晚年多病，故交零落，处境艰难，心中充满失意之感和哀伤之情。这首《孤雁》，表达的就是乱离漂泊中孤独之人的痛苦心情。开篇即唤出"孤雁"，不饮，不啄，只是不断追寻，寻找它的同伴。孤雁还有诗人怜惜，形单影只如同孤雁的诗人又有谁来怜惜呢？诗人与孤雁，浑然一体。清人朱鹤龄评注这首诗说："此托孤雁以念兄弟也"，不只是兄弟，诗人念的还包括

A Lonely Swan

A lonely swan cares not for what it drinks
Singing all the way, for the flock it thinks.
Who will pity its lonely shadow far
Away from the flock as cloud from a star?
It still remains in view though lost to sight,
Its sorrow can be heard in its long flight.
Unlike the insensible duck or crow
Making loud noises in weal as in woe.

了解他懂得他的知音。第三联紧承上联，望断天涯路，仿佛同伴依稀可辨，于是它更要不停地追飞，不停地呼唤了，这两句字字血泪，情深意切，哀痛欲绝。它的心情是那么迫切，而野鸦却全然不懂，“无意绪”是孤雁对着野鸦时的心情，也是杜甫既不能与知己亲朋相见，又要面对着一些俗客庸夫时厌恶无聊的心绪。诗人用诚挚而热烈的感情，抒发了对忠贞之鸟的赞扬之情，也是诗人对自己准则的宣扬。

又呈吴郎

堂前扑枣[①]任西邻，
无食无儿一妇人。
不为[②]困穷宁有此？
只缘[③]恐惧转须亲[④]。
即防远客虽多事，
便插疏篱[⑤]却甚真。
已诉征求贫到骨，
正思戎马泪盈巾。

① 扑枣：把枣子打落下来。

② 不为：如果不是，若非。

③ 只缘：正因为。

④ 转须亲：反而更应该亲近她。

⑤ 插疏篱：稀稀疏疏地修建了一些篱笆。

公元767年，杜甫住在瀼西的草堂里。草堂前有几棵枣树，西邻的一个寡妇常来打枣，杜甫从不干涉。后来，杜甫把草堂让给一位姓吴的亲戚，他自己搬到离草堂十几里路远的东屯去。不料这姓吴的一来就在草堂插上篱笆，禁止打枣。寡妇向杜甫诉苦，杜甫便写此诗去劝告吴郎。吴郎的年辈要比杜甫小，而诗人有意地用了"呈"这个不大相称的敬词，这是让吴郎易于接受。全诗措词十分委婉含蓄，因为诗人希望吴郎接受劝告。说明诗人十分同情体谅穷苦人的处境。在这种委婉曲折中，诗人联想到国家大局，以至流下热泪。这首诗作表达了杜甫对穷困人民的深切同情。

For the Tenant of My Thatched Hall

Let your west neighbor pick up dates before the hall!
A sonless woman now in want of food and all.
Could she pick dates if she were not poor to excess?
You should be kind to her to make her fear you less.
She might be over cautious to be kept away.
Why should you put up a fence in your neighbor's way?
Stricken to the bones, so pitiable she appears.
Thinking of the war flames, how can I not shed tears!

九　日

（五首其一）

重阳独酌杯中酒，
抱病[①]起登江上台。
竹叶于人既无分，
菊花从此不须开。
殊方日落玄猿哭，
旧国霜前白雁来。
弟妹萧条各何在？
干戈[②]衰谢两相催！

① 抱病：生病，带病。

② 干戈：战争。

公元767年重阳，杜甫在夔州登高，有此诗篇。重阳有登高怀远的风俗，诗人抱病前往，应是心中愁绪无法排解。因病戒酒，遂也无心赏菊，用带着较强烈主观情绪的诗句，加强情感表达，胸中不快之意呼之欲出。竹叶，即竹叶青，指代酒。颈联因景伤情，日落猿啼，似乎它们也有胸臆难平之事；白雁归来，尚能与家人团聚。这些，很自然地透露了诗人内心的情绪。尾联以佳节思亲作结，遥怜弟妹，寄托飘零寥落之感，叹息岁月已经催人老，又何苦再以干戈摧残。

On Mountain-climbing Day

(I)

I drink my wine alone on Mountain-climbing Day,
Though ill, I go up riverside tower and stay.
I cannot drink wine made out of bamboo's green leaves;
Chrysanthemums not in full bloom, I think none grieves.
But black apes wail at sunset in a foreign land;
White swans will come before the frost without command.
Where are my homesick younger brothers and sisters dear?
War flames afar and nearing old age make me drear.

登高

风急天高猿啸哀[①]，
渚[②]清沙白鸟飞回。
无边落木萧萧[③]下，
不尽长江滚滚来。
万里悲秋常作客，
百年多病独登台。
艰难苦恨繁[④]霜鬓[⑤]，
潦倒新停浊酒杯。

① 哀：忧愁。

② 渚（zhǔ）：水中的小片陆地。

③ 萧萧：类似风吹动树叶的声音。

④ 繁：增多。

⑤ 霜鬓：白发。

《登高》是杜甫于公元767年秋天在夔州时的杰作，被誉为古今七言律诗之冠。诗的前半写景，后半抒情。第一联刻画眼前具体景物，形声色态，一一得到表现，天风沙渚，自然成对。不但上下两句对，而且还有句中自对，如上句“天”对“风”、“高”对“急”，下句“沙”对“渚”、“白”对“清”，读来富有节奏感。第二联表现了夔州秋天的典型特征。诗人仰望茫无边际、萧萧而下的木叶，俯视奔流不息、滚滚而来的江水，抒发了韶光易逝、壮志难酬的感慨，把眼前景和心中情紧密地

On the Height

The wind so swift, the sky so wide, apes wail and cry;
Water so clear and beach so white, birds wheel and fly.
The boundless forest sheds its leaves shower by shower;
The endless river rolls its waves hour after hour.
A thousand miles from home, I'm grieved at autumn's plight;
Ill now and then for years, alone I'm on this height.
Living in times so hard, at frosted hair I pine;
Cast down by poverty, I have to give up wine.

联系起来了。第三联写诗人漂泊无定的生涯，沦落他乡、年老多病的处境，产生了无限悲愁的情绪。这种情绪从空间（万里悲秋）和时间（百年多病）两方面来表达，诗意显得更加深沉。最后一联作结，诗人备尝艰难潦倒之苦，白发日多，加上因病断酒，悲愁就更难排遣。这种悲愁就像江水和落叶一样，无穷无尽，无边无际，仿佛充塞宇宙，要使万物同声一哭了。古人认为这诗不止“全篇可法”，而且“用句用字”“皆古今人必不敢道，决不能道者”，所以是当之无愧的“旷代之作”。

漫成一首

江月去人只数尺，
风灯[1]照夜欲三更。
沙头宿鹭联拳静，
船尾跳鱼拨剌[2]鸣。

① 风灯：防风的灯。

② 拨剌：象声词。指鱼尾拨动水的声音。

这首诗是公元766年杜甫流寓巴蜀时期，在从云安前往夔州的船上所作。诗写夜泊之景，一开篇便描画了一幅碧波荡漾、月影摇曳、江天一色的夜景图，营造出一种静谧的气氛。被微风吹动摇曳的灯火将夜照得朦胧，恍惚中看见白鹭蜷曲着身子，三五成群地栖息在沙滩上，那样安静恬适。船尾旁有鱼跃出水面，暂时打破了这宁静，以声音结尾，有“蝉噪林逾静，鸟鸣山更幽”之妙。本诗平和静谧，生气灵动，可见诗人对自然与生命的热爱。

Mooring at Night

The moon in the river but a few feet away,
The lantern waits at midnight for the dawning day.
On the beach white egrets fall wing to wing in sleep,
Astern a fish is heard out of water splash and leap.

短歌行赠王郎司直

王郎酒酣拔剑斫地[①]歌莫哀!
我能拔尔抑塞[②]磊落之奇才。
豫章翻风白日动,
鲸鱼跋浪沧溟[③]开。
且脱佩剑休徘徊[④]。
西得诸侯棹[⑤]锦水,
欲向何门趿[⑥]珠履?
仲宣楼头春色深,
青眼高歌望吾子。
眼中之人吾老矣!

① 斫(zhuó)地:砍地。

② 抑塞:郁闷,压抑。

③ 沧溟(míng):大海。

④ 休徘徊:不要犹豫不决。

⑤ 棹(zhào):划船的工具,此处泛指船。

⑥ 趿:拖着鞋子。

这首诗作于公元768年,诗人到达江陵后的春末。上半首表达劝慰王郎之意。王郎在江陵不得志,趁着酒兴正浓,拔剑起舞,斫地悲歌,杜甫劝他不要悲哀。当时王郎正要西行入蜀,杜甫久居四川,表示可以替王郎推荐,所以说“我能拔尔”,把你这俊伟不凡的奇才从压抑苦闷中解脱出

For a Young Friend

My dear drunken young friend,
You draw your sword to strike the ground and sing your plaint.
I can help you to end
Your grief and develop your talent without restraint.
You are a giant tree on which sunbeams would quiver,
Or a leviathan whale to make upsurge a river.
So why should you strike the ground with your sword and shiver?
If you go west to cross the River of Brocade,
On whose door would you lean and on whose balustrade?
The tower for talents is built in vernal hue,
All longing eyes are singing and waiting for you,
Bit in your eyes I'm an old man. What can I do?

来，并盛赞王郎的杰出才能。下半首抒写送行之情。诗人说以王郎的奇才，此去西川，一定会得到高官的赏识，却不知要投在谁的门下。诗人对王郎青眼有加，故高歌寄予厚望，并叹道：你正值青春，前途不可限量，不像我，已经老了。抒发自己才不得施的无奈和悲凉，也含有劝诫王郎之意。

江　上

江上日多雨，
萧萧荆楚[1]秋。
高风下木叶，
永夜[2]揽貂裘。
勋业[3]频看镜，
行藏独倚楼。
时危思报主，
衰谢不能休。

① 荆楚：今湖北省。

② 永夜：长夜。

③ 勋业：功业。

《金圣叹选批杜诗》中说：“《江上》乃是全题，盖身在江上，而心不忘魏阙也。”所谓魏阙，就是皇帝的京城。诗人看见江南多雨，潇潇洒洒，西风一吹，落叶纷纷，他通宵不眠，拥裘独坐，想到事业无成，揽镜自照，容颜已老，长年不为朝廷所用，只好凭栏远望，寄托报国之心。时局危难，自己虽然年事已高，还是欲罢不能，由此可以看出诗人忧国忧民的情怀。

On the River

Each day upon the river falls cold rain;
The southern land in autumn looks forlorn,
The high wind blows down withered leaves again;
All night long I sit in my furs outworn.
No deeds achieved, in mirror oft I frown;
Unused for long, I lean on balustrade.
At this critical hour I'd serve the crown.
Though feeble, can I give up and evade?

江　汉

江汉思归客，
乾坤一腐儒[1]。
片云天共远，
永夜月同孤。
落日[2]心犹壮，
秋风病欲苏[3]。
古来存[4]老马[5]，
不必取长途。

①腐儒：诗人的自称，自嘲。

②落日：垂暮之年。

③病欲苏：病体快要康复。

④存：留养。

⑤老马：诗人自比。

公元768年正月，杜甫自夔州出三峡，流寓江陵等地，写了《江汉》一诗。诗人思归而不能归，成了天涯沦落人。在天地之间，犹如白云一样遥远，仿佛夜月一样孤独。虽然到了夕阳晚境，但是心还未老；西风一起，病体反倒复苏了。他感到自己像识途的老马，尽管无力再走长途，但还是可供驱驰的。这首《江汉》抒发了诗人怀才见弃的不平之气和报国思用的怀抱，情景交融，有强烈的艺术感染力。

On River Han

On River Han my home thoughts fly,
Bookworm with worldly ways in fright.
The cloud and I share the vast sky;
I'm lonely as the moon all night,
My heart won't sink with sinking sun;
Autumn wind blows illness away.
A jaded horse may not have done,
Though it cannot go a long way.

登岳阳楼

昔[①]闻洞庭水，
今上岳阳楼。
吴楚东南坼[②]，
乾坤日夜浮。
亲朋无一字[③]，
老病有孤舟。
戎马关山北，
凭轩[④]涕泗流。

① 昔：从前。

② 坼（chè）：分开。

③ 无一字：没有书信。

④ 凭轩：靠着窗户。

公元 768 年冬天，杜甫由湖北的江陵漂泊到湖南的岳州，写了《登岳阳楼》一诗。前半写景，说诗人早就听说洞庭湖乃天下胜境，但是直到晚年才登上岳阳楼。他看见广阔的湖水把古代吴国和楚国的疆界分开，日月星辰似乎都漂浮在水中。诗的后半述怀：亲友都没有音信，只有年老多病的诗人，泛着一叶扁舟，在江南漂流。眼看万里关山兵荒马乱，诗人只能倚着栏杆涕泗滂沱，声泪俱下。这首诗意境宽阔宏伟，前无古人，后无来者。

On Yueyang Tower

Long have I heard of Dongting Lake,
Now I ascend the Yueyang Height.
Here eastern state and southern break;
Here sun and moon float day and night.
No word from friends or kinsfolk dear,
A boat bears my declining years.
War's raging on the northern frontier,
Leaning on rails, I shed sad tears.

南　征

春岸桃花水[1]，
云帆[2]枫树林。
偷生长避地[3]，
适远更沾襟。
老病南征日，
君恩北望心。
百年[4]歌自苦，
未见有知音。

① 桃花水：形容春天桃花盛开的时节的春潮。

② 云帆：白帆。

③ 避地：前往异乡避难。

④ 百年：一生。

公元769年春，杜甫在由岳阳往长沙的途中作此诗。首联描绘了明媚春光中，一幅美好的自然图景。然而诗人长年颠沛流离，远适南国的羁旅悲愁，更兼光景无多，前路漫漫，触景伤情，这美好春光竟也饱含离愁别绪。诗人北归不得，只能南下，但即使这样，诗人拳拳之心，仍思望报效朝廷。可叹命运弄人，诗人在“春华无人赏”的叹息中老去，却始终无人理解，这是诗人一生的悲剧。

Journey to the South

Peach blossoms in full bloom by riverside,
Cloud-like sails pass by maples far and wide.
To earn a living I have to change place,
Coming from afar, tears stream on my face.
On southern journey, old and ill I sigh;
Looking northward, I long for royal sky.
Why should I torture myself for so long?
Where is the connoisseur who knows my song?

小寒食[1]舟中作

① 小寒食：指清明节的前一天。

佳辰强饮食犹寒，
隐几萧条戴鹖冠。
春水船如天上坐，
老年花似雾中看。
娟娟戏蝶过闲幔，
片片轻鸥下急湍。
云白山青万余里，
愁看直北[2]是长安。

② 直北：正北方。

公元770年寒食节后一天，杜甫在潭州（今长沙）淹留，写了这首《小寒食舟中作》。从寒食到清明三天禁火，诗人只能吃点冷食，勉强喝了点酒。他戴着隐士帽，百无聊赖地在舟中靠茶几坐着。看见春来水涨，江流浩漫，小舟漂荡起伏，犹如身在天上云间；老眼昏花，岸边花草看来如隔薄雾。舟中布幔闲卷，蝴蝶翩跹穿空而过；片片白鸥，轻快地逐流飞翔。作者思绪随着万里不断的云山远去，想到万方多难的长安，不禁忧愁涌上心头。这是杜甫在逝世前半年所作的一首情景交融的七言律诗。

Boating after Cold Food Day

I try to drink, but food's still cold on festive day;
In hermit's cap, at table, drear and bleak I stay.
My boat is drifting on above a mirrored sky,
The flowers look veiled in mist to wrinkled eye.
The listless curtains see butterflies dancing past;
Over the rapids gulls on gulls are skimming fast.
For miles and miles outspread cloud on cloud, hill on hill,
But the imperial town lies farther northward still.

发潭州[①]

夜醉长沙酒，
晓行湘水[②]春。
岸花飞送客，
樯燕[③]语留人。
贾傅才未有，
褚公[④]书绝伦。
名高前后事，
回首一伤神。

① 潭州：地名，今湖南长沙一带。

② 湘水：湘江。

③ 樯燕：立在船桅之上的燕子。

④ 贾傅、褚公：即汉代贾谊和唐代褚遂良。

诗人因时局动乱，亲友尽疏，北归无望，只能泛舟漂泊。公元769年春，诗人离开潭州赴衡州，作此诗。北归无望，前途渺茫，天涯飘零，客居舟中，这都是诗人所忧所愁，无可奈何下只有借酒消愁，沉醉而眠，天明之后，又不得不继续漂泊沦落。首联即流露无限辛酸。颔联从侧面抒发“世情薄，人情恶”的喟叹，然而诗人似乎不太在意这些：自有岸边飞花送我，桅上春燕殷勤留我。让诗人百感交集的，是他想到的被贬长沙的贾谊，和被贬潭州的书法名家褚遂良。历史上才智之士的命运何其相似，这让同样身处湘地的诗人情何以堪！于是诗人产生了情感的共鸣，所有的悲愤忧愁，所有的黯然神伤，都化作一句“往事哪堪回首”。

Departure from Changsha

Drunken at night in Southern town,
I sail on vernal stream at dawn.
Fallen petals bid me adieu,
Swallows' songs retain me anew.
A talent exiled long ago,
A good hand banished in woe.
What good to win a wide-spread fame?
Looking back, nothing's left to blame.

燕子来舟中作

湖南为客动经春，
燕子衔泥两度新[①]。
旧入故园尝识主，
如今社日远看人。
可怜处处巢居室[②]，
何异飘飘托此身[③]？
暂语船樯还起去，
穿花贴水益沾巾[④]。

① 两度新：到现在已是第二个春天，第二次见到燕子衔泥。

② 巢居室：燕子在屋子梁上筑巢。

③ 托此身：到处流浪，寻求安身之处。

④ 沾巾：落泪。此处指作者因感动于燕子多情而落泪。

公元 769 年正月，诗人由岳州到潭州，写这首诗时，已经是第二年的春天了，诗人仍在潭州，客居舟上。时值燕子衔泥的春季，诗人生命将尽，经一春则少一春，故此诗弥漫出一片萧索、苍凉、悲怆的身世之慨。旧时故园燕，所以“尝识主”，如今远看人，大约是因为变化之大不敢相认。想到燕子“处处无家处处家”，诗人顿生“同是天涯沦落人”之感。燕子飞入舟中，寥寥数语而去，继续飘零此生，又不忍径去，穿花贴水，徘徊顾恋，似在惜别，诗人禁不住老泪纵横。全诗极写漂泊动荡的忧思，满是凄怆悲楚，字字血泪。

To Swallows Coming to My Boat

It is the second spring I stay on Southern shore,

To build their nest, the swallows peck twice clods of clay.

"Friends to my garden, you should have known me before.

Why should you gaze at me on this festive spring day?

It is a pity you should build nest here or there.

Does it not look like my boat floating far and nigh?

I should tell you to leave the mast without your stare.

Don't wrinkle the water and bring tears to my eye!"

江南逢李龟年[①]

① 李龟年：唐代著名音乐家。

岐王[②]宅里寻常见，
崔九[③]堂前几度闻。
正是江南好风景，
落花时节又逢君。

② 岐王：唐玄宗的弟弟李范。

③ 崔九：崔涤，唐玄宗时期大臣。

这是杜甫绝句中情感最深沉、含蕴最丰富的一首。李龟年是开元盛世最著名的乐师，经常出入王公贵族之门，如岐王李范宫邸、宠臣崔九宅院。杜甫也因才华卓著受到公侯接待，二人曾经几度相会。但是安史之乱后，二人流落江南，又在潭州相逢，不免感慨系之。江南风景虽好，却成了乱离时世和沉沦身世的反衬。从时间上来讲，已是落花时节；从李龟年来讲，他流落街头，沿街卖唱，“每逢良辰胜景，为人歌数阕，座中闻之，莫不掩泣罢酒”，这是他的落花时节；从杜甫来讲，他年老多病，漂泊江湖，也是他的落花时节；从唐王朝来讲，歌舞升平的盛世成了兵荒马乱的年代，不能不算是它的落花时节。所以“落花时节”四字，总结了40年的时代沧桑、人生变迁，含蕴非常丰富，感慨非常深远。半年之后，杜甫就离开了人世。

Coming across a Disfavored Court Musician on the Southern Shore of the Yangtze River

How oft in princely mansions did we meet!
As oft in lordly halls I heard you sing.
Now the Southern scenery is most sweet,
But I meet you again in parting spring.

图书在版编目（CIP）数据

许渊冲译杜甫诗选：汉文，英文 /（唐）杜甫著；许渊冲编译. --北京：中译出版社，2021.1（2022.7重印）
（许渊冲英译作品）
ISBN 978-7-5001-6451-7

Ⅰ.①许… Ⅱ.①杜… ②许… Ⅲ.①杜诗－诗集－汉、英 Ⅳ.①I222.742

中国版本图书馆CIP数据核字（2020）第240379号

出版发行 中译出版社
地　　址 北京市西城区新街口外大街28号普天德胜大厦主楼4层
电　　话 （010）68359719
邮　　编 100088
电子邮箱 book@ctph.com.cn
网　　址 http://www.ctph.com.cn

出 版 人 乔卫兵
总 策 划 刘永淳
责任编辑 刘香玲　张　旭
文字编辑 王秋璎　张莞嘉　赵浠彤
营销编辑 毕竞方

赏　　析 李　旻
封面制作 刘　哲
内文制作 黄　浩　北京竹页文化传媒有限公司
印　　刷 天津新华印务有限公司
经　　销 新华书店

规　　格 840mm×1092mm　1/32
印　　张 8
字　　数 200千
版　　次 2021年1月第1版
印　　次 2022年7月第3次

ISBN 978-7-5001-6451-7　定价：46.00元